THE TEXAS TATTLER

All The News You Need To Know...And More!

Who remembers four years back, when Texas mogul Kevin Novak was happily married? Didn't think there were many of us. But one has to recall the fervor of the rumor mills when his wife decided to leave her billionaire breadwinner. Everyone was taking bets to see who'd become the next Mrs. Novak.

Except that was not an option—for anyone. The Novaks never divorced. Did the powerful Texas Cattleman's Club member refuse to finalize their estrangement? Or did he always have something else in mind? (He is brilliant, after all.) Because the little missus has finally returned!

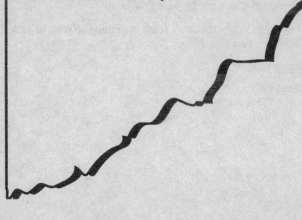

Dear Reader,

I'm so glad to have been invited to write *Texan's Wedding-Night Wager* as part of the TEXAS CATTLEMAN'S CLUB series along with five other fabulous authors.

Set in the fictional town of Somerset, just outside of Houston, my story features dynamic, handsome Kevin Novak (think David Beckham) and his beautiful, feisty, soon-to-be ex-wife, Cara. It's a story of true love and second chances. The two have been separated by distance and regret for four years, and when Cara returns to her hometown to get a divorce, Kevin turns the tables on her.

That's when the fun begins in Maverick County! While Kevin snares Cara in his trap, he becomes a victim of intense attraction and admiration for the wife who abandoned him early in their marriage.

I hope you enjoy the story from beginning to end. In fact, I'll *wager* that you do.

Happy reading!

Charlene

CHARLENE SANDS

TEXAN'S WEDDING-NIGHT WAGER

Published by Silhouette Books
America's Publisher of Contemporary Romance

Special thanks and acknowledgment to Charlene Sands
for her contribution to the Texas Cattleman's Club:
Maverick County Millionaires miniseries.

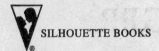

SILHOUETTE BOOKS

ISBN-13: 978-0-373-76964-3

TEXAN'S WEDDING-NIGHT WAGER

Recycling programs
for this product may
not exist in your area.

Visit Silhouette Books at www.eHarlequin.com

Printed in U.S.A.

CHARLENE SANDS

resides in Southern California with her husband, high-school sweetheart and best friend, Don. Proudly, they boast that their children, Jason and Nikki, have earned their college degrees. The "empty nesters" now enjoy spending time together on Pacific beaches, playing tennis and going to movies, when they are not busy at work, of course!

A proud member of Romance Writers of America, Charlene has written twenty-five romance novels and is the recipient of the 2006 National Readers' Choice Award, the 2007 Cataromance Reviewer's Choice Award and the 2008 Booksellers Best Award. Recently *Romantic Times BOOKreviews* magazine nominated her book *Do Not Disturb Until Christmas* as the Best Silhouette Desire of 2008.

Charlene invites you to visit her Web sites www.charlenesands.com, www.petticoatsandpistols.com and www.myspace.com/charlenesands, to enter her contests, check out her new releases and see what's up.

This book is dedicated to all of my friends
and fellow authors on Petticoats and Pistols.
I've never met a smarter, more wonderful, more
gregarious group of authors. Thanks to Pam Crooks,
Stacey Kayne, Cheryl St.John, Kate Bridges,
Linda Broday, Mary Connealy, Pat Potter, Karen Kay
and Elizabeth Lane for being great Western blog pardners.
Y'all make it fun!

Texas Cattleman's Club

One

Cara shut down the ballroom lights and stood in the middle of the floor of Dancing Lights, flanked by a wall of mirrors and elegant surroundings that she'd insisted upon when designing her studios. A smile emerged just as Elton John's voice carried over the speakers. The song stirred up vivid memories and Cara slowly closed her eyes. She moved her hips, swaying to the rhythm and the poetic lyrics.

There's a calm surrender to the rush of day
When the heat of the rolling world can be turned away

An enchanted moment, and it sees me through
It's enough for this restless warrior just to be
with you

And can you feel the love tonight
It is where we are
It's enough for this wide-eyed wanderer
That we got this far
And can you feel the love tonight

"Can you feel the love, Cara?" Kevin had said to her the day they'd married.

Kevin had brought her hand to his mouth and nibbled, his dark blue eyes piercing hers. She'd tingled with excitement from that single gesture. Cara *had* felt his love, with every heart-stopping glance, every tender touch and each tantalizing kiss.

"Yes, I feel it, honey," she'd replied.

He'd kissed her lips, whispering, "This is our song, babe."

They'd hung on to each other and sung the lyrics along with Elton's smooth tones, moving to the music as their family and friends looked on. She thought she'd married her Prince Charming, her college sweetheart who could make her laugh one moment and sizzle the next.

Cara's heart swelled thinking back on her wedding day, thinking of being in Kevin's arms, of loving him for all she was worth and hoping for the same kind of happy life she'd wished for so many of her dance students through the years.

She'd had such big dreams.

"Why, Kevin?" she whispered in the silence of the Dallas ballroom.

Gorgeous Kevin Novak, with the penetrating blue eyes and short blond hair, had often been mistaken for David Beckham. She and Kevin had their own private joke about it since, with her curly blond hair and sky-blue eyes, she hardly looked like Posh Spice. Cara smiled briefly at the memory.

They'd had such good times in the beginning, until Kevin had decided building his real estate empire was more important than building their marriage. He'd become a die-hard workaholic, neglecting her needs in favor of the next big deal. He'd broken her heart—hearing their song again brought it all back. The happiness she'd hoped for with Kevin had eluded them. Cara still felt the ache in the pit of her stomach.

She'd moved on with her life, leaving Somerset to start a new life in Dallas, but she hadn't escaped the deep hurt and anguish Kevin had caused.

Cara snapped her eyes open and stared at the fading shadows in the mirror. Her silhouette reflected back the new, confident woman she'd become. She was a businesswoman now, owner of a chain of dance studios, and a choreographer and dance instructor as well.

No longer that optimistic, hope-filled girl who'd wanted a life and children with Kevin, it was long past time for Cara to rectify her situation.

She punched off the CD player and headed to the

phone to call the man she hadn't spoken with in over four years. She'd waltzed around this issue long enough.

It was time to divorce her husband.

Kevin Novak chalked the cue stick with slow, deliberate twists, contemplating his next shot. He was one of the best pool players at the Texas Cattleman's Club, but his pal Darius Franklin was making him sweat for the win. "You know darn well Montoya is responsible for setting the fire."

Kevin bent over the carved-oak vintage pool table and took his shot, the solid orange cue ball angling into the corner pocket. He knew darn well Darius didn't believe Alejandro Montoya was responsible for the damaging blaze set at Brody Oil and Gas. But he wasn't above using distraction to earn a win.

"I don't know that for a fact, Kev. The fire was definitely an act of arson, but I'm not pointing fingers yet."

"Montoya has always been a pain in the ass."

Kevin missed his next shot and Darius lifted his cue stick, eyeing the pool table. "True, but arson? That's an accusation I'm not ready to make. It looks like a professional job and if that's the case, I'd have to rule him out."

"I say he's guilty." Lance Brody, another of Kevin's old frat brothers from the University of Texas, chimed in. Kevin's four best friends were all members of Texas Cattleman's Club in Maverick

County. They watched the game, sipping drinks and cajoling from the sidelines of the club's game room.

"I'm with Lance," Mitch Brody said, agreeing with his brother. "Montoya's got an ax to grind."

Justin Dupree nodded, taking a swig of beer. "I think Montoya is guilty, too. He's got issues with Lance. Always has."

Lance scoffed. "*I* have issues with him." Their rivalry went back to high-school days.

Darius eyed the striped blue ball and took his shot. The ball rolled into the side pocket and Kevin winced.

"Nice shot."

Darius laughed. "It hurt you to say that, didn't it?"

"Like a knife in my heart."

Darius shook his head. "You're a sore loser, Kev."

"I haven't lost yet."

And when Darius missed his next shot, Kevin went full throttle, unwilling to give an inch. His competitive nature wouldn't allow a loss. He sank the next four solid-color balls, then the eight ball, winning the game.

Satisfied, Kevin shook his friend's hand. "You gave me a run for my money."

Darius slapped a twenty in his palm. "I'll get you next time." He lowered his voice, setting his cue stick into its case. "So you really think Montoya set the fire?"

"I'm thinking he did. I also think he's behind blocking my project in downtown Somerset. He's got it in for the Brody brothers and their friends. Wasn't a coincidence to find the area I'd designated for a major development is being declared an historic district. He's got to be behind the rezoning. It's all a little too suspicious."

Lance walked up and put his arms around their shoulders. "Come on, you two. Let's forget about Montoya for a minute. We need to set a date for my wedding reception. Kate deserves more than the Las Vegas elopement she got."

Kevin grinned. "Yeah, you really know how to impress a girl."

Justin added, "Lance really pulled out all the stops on that one."

"Funny, guys." Lance pulled a frown, but Kevin knew he didn't mind their teasing. He'd found his soul mate in Kate and wanted to provide her a beautiful reception.

When the game-room phone rang, Lance walked over to pick it up. "Cara? Is it really you? It's good to hear your voice."

Kevin froze. All heads turned his way and he met with four pairs of curious eyes. Emotions washed through his system. A tic worked his jaw while he stood rigid and waited.

"Okay, I'll get him. He's right here." Lance nodded his way, holding the phone up. "It's…Cara. She wants to speak with you."

Kevin strode across the room to take the phone. Before speaking, he turned to look at his friends, and with a quick gesture signaled them to continue playing and butt out.

The guys turned around and Kevin spoke into the receiver. "Cara?"

"Hello, Kevin."

So formal.

God, he hadn't heard her voice in four years. Not once. Not since she'd left him high and dry and made a new life for herself in Dallas. He'd kept up on her through friends and what little he'd read in the newspapers about her successful dance studios.

She sounded the same—sassy if not a little stiff. There was an awkward moment of silence.

"I guess it's time for us to end it," she said.

Images of Cara getting remarried immediately entered his mind. After four years, why else would she call? Had she fallen in love with another man?

Kevin didn't know how he'd feel about that. She'd walked out on him and their marriage. She'd tried to file for divorce but Kevin had sent the papers back to her. He'd given her an ultimatum— if she wanted out, she would have to come back and face him.

"I'm coming to Somerset. I'd like to make an appointment with you to discuss the…divorce."

"Fine." Kevin's lips tightened.

"It's business, Kevin. You should understand that. I need an expansion loan for my studios. The bank recommends… Well, let's face it. We both need to get on with our lives."

It's business.

How many times had he said that to her when he couldn't make it home for dinner? When he'd come in so late that he'd plopped into bed beside her and held her tight until they'd fallen asleep? She'd wanted children and Kevin had asked for her patience. His business had come first, but only because he'd wanted to provide a good life for her. He'd made his millions, but she never understood that he'd done it all for her. And how had she showed him her undying love? She'd packed up in the middle of the night and left him. Just like that. After five years of marriage.

Damn her.

"I'm good with that," he said. "When are you coming in?"

"Tomorrow?"

Kevin turned to find all four of his friends silently watching him. "Tomorrow is good. Meet me at the office at five."

Kevin hung up the phone and contemplated his next move. Cara wasn't going to get away with breezing into his life for a day to get her divorce. No, he wouldn't make it so easy for her.

A plan began to formulate in his head and his lips lifted. "Cara's coming to town tomorrow," he said needlessly. "She wants to finalize the divorce."

"I've seen that expression on your face before," Darius said. "What's got you looking so damn smug?"

"Nothing," he replied innocently.

"Like the nothing that nearly got us expelled from UT? Remember when we stole Professor Turner's prized Shakespeare bust from his classroom?" Lance asked, narrowing his eyes. "That kind of nothing?"

Kevin shrugged.

"I don't like it," Lance said. "You looked fit to be tied when she called, and now you're looking like a fat cat who just lapped up a pint of milk."

Kevin only smiled and finished his beer. "I'd better get going."

"I feel for Cara already. That girl won't know what hit her," Darius added.

Kevin walked to the door of the game room, shaking his head. "That *girl* is my *wife*. And she deserves everything she gets."

Darius shot him a warning look. "I always liked Cara."

"Yeah," Kevin said on a deep breath, before exiting the room. "So did I."

As the elevator closed to take Cara up to Kevin's office, she caught sight of herself in the doors' reflective surface. She must have glanced in the mirror a dozen times before leaving her Houston hotel room, making sure she looked just right for her meeting with Kevin. On any given day she wore her curly blond hair pulled back in a clip, but today she let the curls fall to her shoulders freely, glossed her lips with a light berry shade and made sure she wore a soft sapphire dress that accented her figure and her blue eyes.

Because it wasn't any given day.

Today, she'd see her husband for the first time in four years.

And a small part of her wanted him to see what he'd thrown away. She hadn't wilted like a delicate flower when they'd separated. She'd been broken but not beaten by his betrayal of trust. He hadn't cheated on her in the classic way, but he had shattered his vows by abandoning their love.

Cara had grown from that experience. Through her pain, she'd managed to create a successful business in a field she loved. She'd come here for Dancing Lights and that expansion loan she needed from the bank, but she'd also come for her own personal reasons.

She drew oxygen in as she exited the elevator and glanced around Kevin's new office space. He'd certainly come up in the world, from his smaller office on the outskirts of Houston to this impressive space on the tenth floor of a downtown high-rise building.

She walked to the reception desk and waited for the receptionist to finish her phone call.

"May I help you?" she asked.

"Yes, I'm Mrs. Novak. I have an appointment… with my husband."

The young woman's eyebrows shot up, surprise evident on her face. Kevin had replaced a great many things since she'd left and apparently sweet, aging Margie Windmeyer, his loyal secretary, hadn't fit in with the new decor.

Looking baffled, the receptionist paged through her appointment book.

"He's expecting me." Cara's nerves jumped at the edginess in her tone. She wanted to get this over with.

"Yes, Mrs. Novak." The receptionist gave up looking for her name on the books and pointed toward a set of double doors. "Right through there."

Cara nodded and stared at the doors for a second. Then, with her slim briefcase tucked under her arm, she entered the office.

Kevin stood with his back to her, staring out the arched window behind his desk. Both hands tucked into his suit pants, she was treated to a captivating view of his tight backside. His physique hadn't suffered through the years—that much she could determine right away.

As he angled toward her, his profile and the sharp, handsome lines of his face struck her with force. He turned fully around and stared at her, his gorgeous, piercing-blue eyes not giving anything away.

He cast her a half smile. "Cara."

She stood in the middle of the large office, refusing to let her nerves go raw. It was a shock to see him. She couldn't possibly have anticipated this moment—how she'd react to seeing him again. She'd imagined it a hundred times, but nothing compared to the reality. Seeing him brought back bittersweet memories of all they'd had and all they'd lost, which swept through her in a matter of seconds.

She got hold of her bearings and smiled a little. "Hello, Kevin."

Kevin eyed her up and down, the way he used to when he wanted to make love to her. Heat swelled and coursed through her body, a remnant of what they'd once shared coming to light. Suddenly, the enormity of her mission here struck her. She would put an ending note on the last chapter of their marriage.

"You look…well."

Kevin taunted her. "You look *beautiful*."

"Thank you." Cara held on to her defenses, despite the bitter way he offered up the compliment.

"Have a seat, Cara." He gestured and she sat in a brown leather chair facing him.

Cara fidgeted with her briefcase, finally setting it on Kevin's desk. She crossed her legs and tapped her fingers on the arms of the chair.

Kevin's gaze fell to her thighs, where the material of her dress gathered. She refused to squirm under his direct scrutiny. But she wished he'd sit down.

"Are you getting remarried?"

His blunt question surprised her. She shook her head. "No."

He nodded, folding his arms across his rigid body.

"It's just time, Kevin. We need to move on. I'm planning to expand my business and I need to get a large bank loan."

"You don't want my name on anything legal, right?" His eyes narrowed on her.

"You're a businessman," she responded with patience, wondering what happened to the Kevin Novak she'd married. This man seemed so different, so dark and contemptuous. She'd never seen this side of Kevin before. "You know how it works."

"Yeah, I know how it works." His cutting, derisive tone sobered the moment even more.

Kevin finally took a seat behind his desk. He braced his elbows on the chair arms and steepled his fingers. "Don't you find it strange that we're sitting here in my office, speaking formalities?"

"Strange?"

The corner of Kevin's mouth lifted in a wry smile. "Yeah, strange. Considering how we started out. Hot and heavy from the moment we laid eyes on each other."

Cara recalled her college sorority sister's birthday bash, with balloons and loud music and alcohol flowing. She'd taken one look at Kevin and fallen in love instantly. They'd spent the entire night flirting shamelessly. Cara had never been so aware of her own sensuality until that day. She and Kevin had blown off the party. They'd had a party of their own that night.

Heat crawled up her neck at the erotic memory. "That's the past, Kevin."

Kevin let her comment drop. He leaned back in his seat and stared into her eyes. "I understand your dance studios are doing very well."

Cara's heart sped up at his implication. She straightened in her seat and leaned forward a bit. "I'm not here for your money, Kevin." She glanced around the elaborate surroundings. Exquisite Southwest artwork adorned the walls of his very tastefully decorated office. "Though I see you've become a huge success. That was always most important to you."

Cara made her point and leaned back in her seat, content to put a name on the mistress who'd stolen her marriage from her. "I'm only here for your signature."

"And you'll get it," Kevin said.

Oh, boy. That was easy, Cara thought, sighing silently with relief.

"Under one condition. I want something from you, Cara."

So Kevin had terms. She'd be willing to hear him out. She wanted nothing more than to get this whole ordeal over and done with. "I'm willing to do anything, within reason."

Kevin grinned a little too widely. "Considering you abandoned me and our marriage, I think my request is quite reasonable."

Cara went numb. She didn't like the look on her husband's face. "You forced my hand, Kevin. I hung on to our marriage for years, hoping. But you gave me no option—"

"And I'm giving you no option now. If you want your precious divorce," he said, "you'll have to agree to my terms."

Two

Kevin watched Cara's sudden panic when his request finally sank in. Momentarily silenced, Cara blinked rapidly, giving him a chance to really look his wife over.

He hadn't realized what four years of separation had done to him. He'd never met a woman he admired more than Cara, or thought more beautiful or talented. Cara had it all. He'd always thought so, and everything he'd done, he'd done for her. He'd wanted to prove to her and her wealthy family that she'd married well. That he could give her all the things she deserved.

God, how he'd loved her.

Kevin inhaled sharply and Cara's head snapped up. "You can't be serious, Kevin."

"I'm not joking."

Cara stood abruptly and stared straight into his eyes. "No, I don't suppose you have a sense of humor anymore."

He caught a slight whiff of her exotic scent, the same fragrance she'd worn when they'd been truly man and wife. Memories of hot, erotic nights flooded his senses. Of her silky smooth skin against his flesh, her breath against his cheek, her soft, sensual body tucked under his.

He wanted her again. He'd given her no other choice but to accept his demand. He wouldn't let Cara have the last laugh. "On the contrary, babe. I have a great sense of humor, when something is funny. This, however, isn't funny."

"It's ridiculous! You want me to live with you for a week? Why, Kevin?"

Kevin arched his brows, but remained silent.

Her blue eyes sparked like raging fire when she caught on. She shook slightly and pointed her finger. "This is blackmail."

"You owe me for walking out."

Indignant, Cara raised her voice. "You walked out on *us!*"

Kevin's gut tightened. "No, Cara," he said with quiet calm. "I worked hard to give us a good start."

Cara shook her head so hard her blond curls whipped across her face. "No, no, no. I won't let you get away with that. I wanted *you*. I wanted a *family*. *Children*. You only wanted to amass a fortune. You were never there for me, Kevin."

He shrugged. He'd heard this all before and he'd never agreed with her take on their marriage. He'd asked for one thing from Cara—patience. He'd wanted to give her the world. "So your solution was to run away?"

Cara backed up a step and lowered her voice. "I couldn't do it anymore. I needed more from you."

"And leaving Somerset solved the problem for you." Kevin snapped his fingers. "Just like that, you were gone."

A sharp, stinging pain sliced through his gut. Kevin didn't think Cara had the power to hurt him anymore, but seeing her again brought back all the bitter memories. They'd argued the night before Cara had left and had gone to bed angry with each other, but that was nothing compared to the memory of finding that Cara had slipped out of the house before dawn, leaving only a note in her wake.

"It wasn't as easy as you make it seem." Cara's pretty mouth turned down. She filled her lungs with a fortifying breath and opened her slim attaché case, pulling out the divorce papers. "If you'll forget this nonsense and just sign the papers, you and I…"

"Will be done?"

Cara closed her eyes. "Yes. Please, Kevin. This is difficult enough."

She got that right. It was difficult seeing her again. All the old, hurtful feelings came tumbling back. Her leaving had cut him deep and left him bleeding. He'd hidden his injury from those around him until he'd become numb inside, then bitterness had emerged. He'd spent the next few years resenting Cara Pettigrew and trying to wash away her memory with an occasional one-night stand, women who would never measure up. He'd refused relationships and poured all his energy back into his business.

Kevin shrugged off his pain the way he'd learned to, from years of experience. He stood his ground. "I told you, I want one week with you, Cara. One week at my penthouse. And then I'll sign the divorce papers."

Cara's shoulders slumped. She shoved the papers back into the attaché case and snapped it shut. "I can't do that."

Kevin walked around his desk and approached her. Her eyes gleamed like diamonds and her skin appeared soft as a baby's, but it was her very kissable mouth, tight as it was at the moment, that had him moving in even closer. He'd never gotten over his anger with her, but he'd also never gotten over wanting her. And now that she was here, he wanted one last fling with his wife.

Before he ended their marriage for good.

He touched her wrist and slid his finger tenderly up her arm. Goose bumps broke out on her skin and Kevin felt a moment of satisfaction. "If you want the divorce, you're going to have to pay for it."

Breathless, Cara looked deep into his eyes. "You've changed, Kevin."

"I won't deny it."

Cara moved back a step and Kevin dropped his hand from her arm. She worked the inside of her lower lip in that adorable way that always made him hot for her.

"I'll make you a counteroffer."

Kevin smiled inside. He should have known his feisty wife wouldn't give in without a fight. It was a trait he'd always admired about her. "I'm listening."

"One night. You get one night and that's all."

Initially Kevin balked. One night wasn't nearly enough to exact his payback. He wanted more time with her. His plan was to romance her into falling in love with him again. The ultimate revenge for dumping him would be in his rejection of her. Then he'd sign her divorce papers.

A thought struck and Kevin acted swiftly. "You've got a deal. If and only if you agree that our one night will be two weeks from tonight."

"Two weeks? I can't possibly—"

"That's my offer. You stay in town for two weeks, and in exactly fourteen days you'll have your divorce. Take it or walk away now with those unsigned papers, babe."

Cara narrowed her eyes and crinkled her nose. She mulled it over for a few seconds, then finally gave him her uplifted chin. "Fine. But only because I need that bank loan. You've got me up against a wall."

Her scent drew him closer. She looked so darn beautiful when she was indignant. He arched a brow. "Baby, I've *had* you up against a wall. Remember?"

Recollection replaced the surprise on her face and her features softened with the memory. Kevin wrapped his hands around her slender waist and tugged her against him, his fingers splayed across her backside.

"Kevin," she whispered, before his mouth claimed hers.

Kevin could kiss and Cara fell into him for all she was worth. His expert lips teased and tempted her with little nibbles until sizzling heat built up. She tried a vain attempt to pull away, but Kevin only brought her up tighter, pressing her hips to his with a subtle grind that swept through her system. Her knees buckled, her heart slammed as the frenzied kiss overwhelmed her. She found it hard to breathe. And when she opened her mouth to take in oxygen, Kevin mated their tongues and the tantalizing thrill escalated.

He cupped her head in both hands and kissed her again and again, their breathing labored and intense. In the past, this kind of kiss had meant only one thing—a steamy night under the sheets. Kevin could always turn her inside out…

The sobering thought of his blackmail returned full force.

Damn him. Damn him. Damn him.

She didn't want this. She didn't want to be swayed by memories of hot, mind-blowing sex with her husband. She'd put those thoughts out of her mind, for the most part. She'd come here for a signature and instead got a near-orgasmic experience just from one kiss.

She pushed at his chest and broke off the kiss.

Kevin glanced at her lips, which she was sure were red and swollen, and smiled. "Two weeks is gonna be a long time."

"We could finish it here and now." Cara nearly died of mortification when Kevin noticed her glancing at the top of his uncluttered desk.

"Tempting," Kevin said, his gaze raking her over. "But we made a deal."

"Couldn't we undo that deal, Kevin?" She prayed her plea came through sure and steady, instead of desperate.

Kevin stepped away from her and shook his head. "The way you undid our marriage? No, Cara. This time you're not running away from me. In fact, I want you to have dinner with me tomorrow night. I'll pick you up at seven."

Cara jammed her hands on her hips. Who was this man? Certainly, he wasn't the man she'd fallen in love with and married nine years ago. "You can't issue orders like that to me, Kevin. I'm not at your beck and call."

Chagrined, Kevin scratched his head, acknowledging his mistake. "Sorry," he said. "Guess I'm out of practice wining and dining a lady."

His confession touched something deep in her heart. Furious with him as she was, it was nice to know that behind all his anger there was a glimmer of the man she'd once known. And to know that Kevin was out of practice with women instilled great comfort within her.

Kevin made a point of clearing his throat and beginning anew. "Cara, I'd like for you to join me for dinner tomorrow night. We have a lot to catch up on. And I could use your advice about something."

Curious, Cara raised her brows. "My advice?"

"Yes, you always had a level head and you know the parties involved. I want to run something by you. Will you join me for dinner?"

After raising her curiosity level a notch, Cara could hardly refuse. "Yes, okay. I'll have dinner with you. I'm staying at the Four Seasons."

Kevin nodded. "I'll pick you up at seven." He moved to his desk to retrieve her attaché, and without pause laid a hand to her back and walked her to the door. Handing her the briefcase, he looked into her eyes. "I'm looking forward to seeing you tomorrow night, Cara."

Cara nodded, biting her lip to keep from making a snarky retort like, *You're blackmailing me into this. What choice do I have?*

But in fact she did have a choice. She could've made up an excuse not to have dinner with him. Maybe that would have been the wiser move. Yet Cara had been curious, not only about the advice Kevin wanted, but to learn what had become of her friends in Somerset.

After leaving him, she'd lost touch with so many

people and she'd always regretted that. Maybe it was time to renew those friendships while she was here.

Cara bounded out of Kevin's office with a bounce in her step. This wasn't how she'd envisioned her encounter going—especially succumbing to Kevin's kiss the way that she had—but her goals were in sight.

And that was all that mattered to her.

Cara walked the distance to her hotel, willing to trudge the ten blocks in high heels rather than hailing a cab. It was a good way to cool off from Kevin's melt-your-heart kiss and his blatant blackmail. She didn't know which of the two disturbed her more.

She'd had little power over Kevin's kiss. From day one, she'd never been able to resist him. That's why she'd stolen off in the middle of the night four years ago, fearing that if she'd told him her plans he'd convince her to stay. He'd make his argument, as he had so many other times, and kiss her into oblivion.

But she'd thwarted his blackmail attempt. Somewhat. She could take some satisfaction in that. He'd wanted a week with her when it was clear their marriage was over, and she'd offered him *one* night. Some might not think it a victory, but Cara knew how determined Kevin was and his compromise certainly meant a win, small as it might be.

Cara clutched her briefcase and thought of the divorce papers inside. Soon, she'd have the independence she needed to expand her business without relying on her mother's money, which she'd managed to do so far. Since leaving Kevin, she'd looked forward to being her own woman and was proud of her accomplishments. Everything she'd achieved, she'd done on her own. Though her mother had offered to fund her dance studios, Cara wanted to make it on her own. So Cara viewed negotiating with Kevin to get him to sign the divorce papers as a business proposition—a means to achieving her goal.

"Soon, Cara-Bella," she whispered, smiling at the nickname her dance instructors had bestowed upon her, claiming she danced like a princess.

Soon, you'll have what you came here for.

As she moved along the sidewalk, taking in the sights and sounds of downtown Houston, gradually her steps slowed to a stroll. She calmed herself by window-shopping, glancing at the familiar storefronts, noting which had revamped their exteriors and which had gone out of business, replaced by newer, more upbeat trendy shops.

People moved along the sidewalks at a quick pace, but that didn't stop her from spotting Alicia Montoya across the street, bogged down with several shopping bags. She waved, trying to get her attention. "Alicia!"

Alicia swiveled her head and saw her. Surprised, she smiled and waved back, then gestured toward the street corner. Cara met her there after crossing the street.

"Cara, it's so good to see you!" She gave her a double-armed, shopping-bag hug.

Cara chuckled and knew the first moment of actual joy since coming to Houston. She hugged her back. "Alicia, I'm happy to see you, too. It's been years."

She and Alicia had become friends in her first years of marriage with Kevin, despite her brother's objections. Alex Montoya didn't want his family involved with any friends of either Lance or Mitch Brody. Both those men had been close to Kevin since their college days, along with Justin Dupree and Darius Franklin. Alex's extreme hatred carried over to anyone involved with the five men of the Texas Cattleman's Club.

"Yes, it has been. I wish we had stayed in touch," Alicia said quietly.

"I'm really sorry about that, Alicia. I went through a hard time. Leaving my home and everything I knew…wasn't easy. I needed to make a clean break."

Alicia's chocolate-brown eyes softened. "I understand. But you're here now."

"Yes, I'm here for two weeks. I'd actually planned on calling you, so I'm doubly glad I spotted you. Looks like you bought out the store."

Alicia glanced down at the shopping bags she held. "I know, I went a little crazy. I don't shop much, so I had some making up to do. Where are you staying?"

"In a hotel just down the street. Do you think we can get together while I'm here?"

"I was just going to suggest that. We can meet in Somerset for lunch."

"Sounds great." Cara handed Alicia her business card. "Here's my cell number. I'm looking forward to it."

Alicia smiled when she read the card designed with two dancing figures silhouetted by twinkling lights. "Dancing Lights. I like it, Cara. I'd heard you opened a dance studio."

Cara shrugged. "All my gymnastics and cheerleading really paid off, I guess. We teach all kinds of dance at the studio. It keeps me out of trouble."

Thoughtful, Alicia glanced at the card again. "I'll call you at the end of the week. I have to meet Alejandro now. He's expecting me."

Cara nodded. She couldn't send a greeting to Alicia's brother. Not when he'd tried to break up her friendship with Alicia, simply because she'd married Kevin. Guilt by association didn't sit well with her.

"Okay, I'll see you soon. I'm really looking forward to it." The sentiment held true—Cara wanted to renew friendships she'd allowed to dissolve when she'd left town. Alicia was a sweetheart and had lent a compassionate ear to Cara when her marriage had fallen apart. She'd love to get acquainted with her again.

Cara stopped in the food court of the Galleria and picked up an Asian salad for dinner before heading to her hotel. When she entered her room, she kicked off her shoes and sat down on the bed, exhausted from the turmoil of the day.

Not two minutes later, a knock came at her door.

She groaned and lifted herself off the bed. "Yes," she said, opening the door to a hotel employee.

"Mrs. Novak? This came for you. Special delivery."

An "ohh" escaped from Cara before she realized it. The young man handed her a dozen black calla lilies and lavender orchids, beautifully arranged in a vase.

"Thank you," she said and gave him a tip before closing the door. Admiring the lilies, she set them down on the dresser and plucked the card out.

She read the note. "I didn't forget your favorite." Tears stung her eyes for a second. She knew the exotic flowers were from Kevin. Cara had a thing for the unique-colored lilies and it had been the one extravagance she'd requested for their wedding.

Emotion stirred in her stomach and she flopped onto the bed. Staring at the ceiling, her throat constricted and she whispered in the silence of the room, "You didn't forget, did you, Kevin."

Kevin sank the putt and eagled the eighteenth hole, then pumped his fist once, twice, in a fair imitation of Tiger Woods. The TCC's golf course wasn't exactly a tournament course but Kevin was too happy with the turn of events lately to give a damn. He liked winning.

"Lucky shot," Lance muttered with mocking disgust.

"Lucky, my ass. That's pure skill, Brody. That makes five wins to your two, this month."

"I had you beat until those last three holes," Lance

grumbled. "It's as if you can't wait to get off the course today."

At the reminder of time, Kevin glanced at his watch. He had to stop by his office, change and get ready to pick up Cara.

"Got a hot date or something, Kev?" Lance's mouth curled into a smirk.

Kevin set his putter into his golf bag. "I'm seeing Cara tonight."

Lance whistled low and long. "Is there an inkling of hope for you two?"

Kevin glanced at Lance. "Not even a chance."

Lance blinked. "You're saying that you're over her?"

Kevin gritted his teeth. Damn right, he was over her. No matter that seeing her yesterday had reminded him of good times they'd shared or that he looked forward to seeing her again tonight. "Yeah, I'm over her."

"But you're taking her out tonight, right?"

"Yeah, I'm taking her out."

"Hey, just tell me to butt out, buddy. But I saw the look on your face yesterday when she called. You were hopping mad. And anger means you still care. And it also means that you're up to something. I know you, Kevin."

"I'm having one last fling with my wife before I sign the divorce papers," Kevin said in his own defense. "There's no crime in that."

"Unless you have an ulterior motive."

Kevin shrugged. "She'll be here for a couple of weeks." Thanks to his blackmail.

After stowing their bags on the back end of the golf cart, he and Lance settled in the seats, Kevin taking the driver's side.

"So you plan on dating her, and then what?" Lance wouldn't give up.

Kevin stared at him thoughtfully and exhaled. Every one of his friends knew how much Cara had hurt him when she'd left. Though Kevin wouldn't openly admit his plan to anyone, it wouldn't be hard for any one of his friends to put two and two together.

"You're going to win her back and dump her, aren't you?" Lance said, his face twisting in disbelief. When Kevin didn't deny it, Lance shook his head. "Oh, man. Kev, if you have a second chance with someone special, take it. Don't blow it, the way I almost did with Kate."

Kevin tossed Lance's words back at him. "This is the part where I say, butt out, buddy."

He didn't need a lecture. Ever since Lance had married Kate, he seemed to want everyone else to follow suit. Only Kevin wasn't shopping for happily-ever-after anymore. He just wanted a little payback for all the heartache and humiliation Cara had caused him.

"Okay, fine," Lance said. "But don't say I didn't warn you."

Later that day, Kevin went to the office to look over some contracts before sending them to his legal department. He wanted a clear head when he picked up Cara. One of the things he'd learned over the past four years was to surround himself with employees he trusted, and delegate the work. He found that freed up more of his time for pleasurable endeavors, which lately amounted to a round of golf or a game of pool with his buddies.

Anticipation stirred his blood. Cara posed a greater challenge than beating Darius in pool or Lance at golf. And, hell, he had to face facts—he was looking forward to spending his nights with her again.

Just like old times, a voice in his head said.

Kevin left the office at five, drove to his apartment, showered, shaved and checked on the arrangements he'd made for his first date with Cara.

He arrived at her hotel room a little early and knocked on the door.

"Just a minute," she called from inside.

Kevin smiled just hearing the lilt of her sassy voice.

She opened the door wide and whispered, out of breath, "You're early."

She fixed a silver hoop earring to her lobe, looking a little flustered but beautiful all the same in a black silky dress that showed off her long, shapely dancer's legs. Her hair curled past her shoulders and was held up on one side by a crystal clip.

"You look gorgeous, Cara." He stepped into the room.

Cara looked him up and down, surprise registering on her face. And before she could comment on *his* attire, he shook his head and added, "It's a shame you're going to have to take off all your clothes."

Three

Dressed in jeans and wearing leather boots Kevin had provided, Cara sat upon Dream Catcher, the five-year-old mare who had been born at TCC's stables when Cara had been living with Kevin. Though she had grown up with horses on her parents' estate, Cara had forgotten how much she loved riding. She and Kevin had taken an occasional ride in their early years of marriage, before he'd been too obsessed with work to take the time.

The day Dream Catcher was born, Cara had rushed to the stables and the moment she'd seen the feisty little filly, she'd fallen a little bit in love. To sit upon the sweet mare and ride off into the hills of Maverick County with Kevin seemed almost like a dream.

The Texas sun lowered on the horizon and cast hues of orange-gold over the valley as they rode in silence. There was a quiet settle to the land, a peace like nothing Cara had experienced for a long time. She'd been so caught up in the fast pace of Dallas that she'd forgotten what it was like to be with nature. Kevin seemed to understand that, setting the slow pace and enjoying the scenery. There was an odd sense of comfort being here with him. She could almost forget his blackmail and his manipulation.

Almost.

She slid a glance his way and let go a little sigh. Looking just as comfortable atop a horse as he was cutting a deal in his downtown office, Kevin acclimated well. Dressed in solid Wranglers, a blue plaid shirt and black Stetson, her husband dressed down *very* nicely.

"You're staring at me," he said with a grin.

"Oh, you'd like to think so." Caught, Cara averted her gaze, hiding her own grin.

"I know so. See anything you like?"

Cara sobered at his question. "I don't know, Kevin. Do I?"

Kevin clucked his jaw a few times. "You need to lighten up, Cara. Enjoy the scenery."

"And you think you're part of that scenery?"

"Me?" he said, lowering the brim of his hat. "No, ma'am. I wouldn't presume."

Cara chuckled. Okay, maybe she should just lighten up. She didn't like Kevin's blackmail, but she could enjoy the ride. If for no other reason than that she was atop Dream Catcher on a glorious, late-summer evening.

"I see a whole lot I like," Kevin said quietly, after a minute.

Cara sensed his gaze on her, and a burning heat crawled up her neck. She didn't dare look at him. A lump formed in her throat. She didn't trust herself to respond.

They rode in silence until the dirt path led them to a rise. "Wait here," Kevin said mysteriously, and clicked his mare into a trot. He rode on about ten yards to the peak of the rise, then turned toward her. "Okay, come on up." He gestured with a wave.

Dream Catcher followed the path in a trot, until Cara met Kevin at the top of the rise. Looking into his eyes first, then following the direction of his gaze, Cara gasped at the view below. "Oh, Kevin. This is amazing."

A small, well-kept cottage on the TCC property was lit outside by at least a hundred pillar candles. A table, dressed in white linen, was set with fine china, crystal wineglasses and lilies of every variety.

"It's beautiful." Tears stung her eyes. Why couldn't he have done something like this years ago when their marriage was shaky, when she needed attention, when she needed to know she was more important than his business? *Oh, Kevin,* she thought, *why are you doing this now, when it's too late?* The question plagued her, but she pushed it out of her mind.

Lighten up, Cara. This is temporary.

"I'm glad you like it." Kevin pushed his horse on, and Dream Catcher followed him down the other side of the rise. When they reached the cottage, Kevin dismounted. He walked over to Cara and reached for her. She slid down the left side of the horse into Kevin's arms. He held her, their gazes entwined, as luminous candles lit the background.

"You were always gorgeous in candlelight, babe."

Cara smiled, the compliment warming her heart.

Kevin tilted his head, the brim of his Stetson grazing her forehead. She braced herself for the kiss, tightening up inside in anticipation.

Kevin brushed his lips over hers in the lightest feather-touch of a kiss, then backed away. Cara blinked, a little surprised.

He took her hand. "Have a seat." He guided her to the table and pulled out a chair for her. "I'll see to the horses."

She watched him take the reins of both horses and go behind the cottage. When he returned and sat down, a chef appeared at the table wearing a white coat and tall hat, a waiter standing just behind him. "I hope you enjoy the meal Mr. and Mrs. Novak," the chef said.

"I'm sure we will," Kevin returned, with a nod.

Cara sat quietly while the waiter served their first course, a little pastry puff filled with light cheese and raspberries. She took her first bite and closed her eyes. "Oh…this is heaven."

When she opened her eyes, Kevin's gaze was on her, watching her enjoy the pastry with a gleam in his eyes. "The chef came highly recommended."

Cara was again tempted to ask, why was he going to so much trouble? But she'd already decided that she would just go with the flow and see where that would take her, so she remained silent on the subject. "I can see why. He's already got my vote for Chef of the Year."

Kevin poured them each a glass of wine.

"You said something about needing my advice?" Cara sipped her wine and the smooth liquid warmed her inside. "But you haven't said a word about it yet."

Kevin lifted his glass to his lips and sipped. "It's not a pleasant subject, Cara. I hate to spoil the night, but yes, I do have something I'd like to tell you. It's regarding Alex Montoya and the recent fire at Brody Oil and Gas. I think it was set deliberately."

"You think Alex did it?" Cara's voice elevated with disbelief. Sure, the Brody brothers had issues with Alex, and vice versa, from their teen years, but Cara never thought Alejandro Montoya capable of something as criminal as arson.

"I do, Cara. I'd like your opinion about this. Hear me out."

Kevin gave a detailed description of what had transpired between Lance, Mitch and Alex through the years, and then added a final note about how Alex had managed to hamper his newest revitalization development. He explained how Alex had helped back a faction that had that particular area in Somerset declared historic, thus killing the project. "I have no proof regarding the fire, but you know everyone involved. What do you think?"

Cara shook her head. She thought about the accidental meeting she'd had with Alicia just yesterday. Alicia would be devastated if her brother was involved with the fire in any way. "My gut instincts tell me Alex wouldn't do anything so drastic. It's not his style, Kevin. Yes, I can see him behind the scenes, working to preserve the Somerset area. He may have even done that to spite you, but that's not a criminal act."

"No, it just caused me a major headache and financial losses."

"You may not agree with me," she said with a shake of her head, "but I don't think Alex had anything to do with the refinery fire."

"Okay, noted. You and Darius are the only ones. Lance, Mitch, Justin and I all think he's behind it."

Cara sipped her wine. "Maybe you're not being objective. Maybe you want to blame Alex. Maybe you're so pissed at him, you want him to be guilty." Kevin winced and Cara continued. "Revenge can be sweet, isn't that what you always said?"

"No, I never said that."

Cara blinked and leaned forward. "Oh, sorry, that must have been the *other* husband I married nine years ago."

"Must have been." With a smug look, Kevin lifted his glass and finished off his wine. He poured himself another glass as the waiter cleared their dishes and brought the next course.

"So, is that all you wanted to ask me?" Cara dived into her asparagus salad, her appetite flaring to life.

"Yes."

"Are you sorry you asked for my opinion?"

"No." Kevin spoke with an earnest tone. "I always valued your opinion. That hasn't changed."

Cara sat back in her seat and stared into Kevin's eyes. "You can be so charming—when you want to be."

"I want to be. Right now. With you."

Why? Cara didn't understand it, but the voice in her head told her to go with it and enjoy these last few days with Kevin. Soon enough, their marriage would be over.

When they finished all four courses of the main meal, Kevin suggested they go inside the cottage for coffee and dessert. "The chef made us something special."

"I should be full, but I can always fit in dessert," Cara said, feeling the zipper of her jeans expanding a bit. She was slender and, at five foot eight, she could afford to eat a decadent dessert once in a while.

Kevin stood and reached for her hand. With fingers entwined, they entered the cottage, climbing the steps, their boots scraping the wooden floors. Cara made a quick tour of the quaint cottage, noting the rustic stone fireplace, cozy chintz sofa and several swag-draped pane windows. "It's lovely here."

"It was the groundskeeper's home at one time. TCC let it go to ruin, practically. I renovated it and now it's available—"

"For impressing your dates?" she blurted, in a teasing tone.

Kevin whipped around and grabbed her by the waist, bringing her flush up against him. "You have a mouth on you, don't you?"

Cara pulled her head back to look at him fully. "You always liked my sassy mouth."

Kevin's gaze devoured her mouth. He cupped her head with one hand and pulled her close, his lips so near. "I still do."

Cara's heart pumped double time when he kissed her. He tasted of robust wine and warmth. He tasted familiar and fine. He tasted of all the sweet things in her life she missed. "Kevin."

"I love it when you whimper my name," he said between kisses.

"I didn't whimper," Cara protested mildly. Kevin cupped her derriere and tugged her in. Hip jamming hip, she felt his desire, rough against rough as their jeans brushed.

Kevin nibbled on her throat. "Really? Guess I'm gonna have to do something about that."

There were times when Kevin hated his methodical mind and this was one of them. Every instinct he possessed told him to seduce Cara, here and now, and take advantage of the remote, romantic cottage setting. But Kevin had a plan in mind, and the culmination of that plan had to happen later rather than sooner.

He'd kick himself tomorrow for his damnable obstinate nature and pay the price of losing out on a wild night of sex with his wife. Yet all wasn't lost. He needed more from Cara tonight and he'd take what little his plan allowed.

He nipped at Cara's lips over and over, sweeping his tongue through her mouth with frenzied heat. A little tiny moan escaped her throat that sent Kevin's straining erection into overdrive.

With an effort that took all of his will, he pulled away from her to look deep into her eyes. Her hazy-blue surrender unnerved him.

He needed to touch her and feel the softness of her skin, caress the firm mounds of her perfect breasts. Nothing was going to stop him, his plan be damned.

"Baby," he murmured, licking the soft center of her throat. "Let me touch you."

She trembled and whimpered helplessly.

Kevin kissed his way down to the first button of her blouse. With nimble fingers, he undid that button, then the next and the next. Her breasts, cupped in white cotton, spilled out, an invitation he couldn't ignore.

He palmed her breasts and closed his eyes, relishing the remembered feel of her, the way she fit so completely in his hand. His thumbs simultaneously caressed both erect tips, her nipples straining against her bra, until Kevin freed them from the torture.

"Ohh," she moaned, leaning closer to him with a need he knew he couldn't satisfy tonight.

"You feel as good as you look, baby. As good as I remember," he murmured.

Kevin bent his head and kissed the tips of her breasts, first one, then the other. Always responsive to his touch, she arched back and Kevin drew her deep into his mouth, suckling and teasing the rosy buds with his tongue.

He wanted to take her here and now, to ease the desire straining against his jeans, to begin to rectify four years of wanting her, despite his anger. It was hard to back off, to pull away from what she offered and what he wanted, but Kevin was determined to see his plan through.

"Did you hear that?" he asked quietly.

Breathlessly, she replied, "You mean the pounding of my heart?"

Kevin smiled and kissed her lips. "No, outside. Something spooked the horses. I'll go check."

Cara appeared a little surprised by his quick dismissal. He turned and walked out the front door. Behind the house, the horses calmly waited. Kevin leaned against the cottage wall, beside a hibiscus vine in full yellow bloom, and shut his eyes. "Harder than I thought," he whispered.

He waited just a few moments, until his breathing slowed and his internal thermostat cooled down. Then he untied the reins of both horses and guided them toward the front of the cottage. Cara waited on the porch steps. "False alarm," he said. "Must have just been a coyote howl off in the distance."

Thankfully, Cara had buttoned her blouse and straightened her unruly, honey-blond hair. He only had so much willpower where his wife was concerned. He tilted his head and sighed, without falsity. "We should go. It's getting late."

Cara blinked a few times, then nodded. "Of course."

Kevin helped Cara onto Dream Catcher and then bounded up onto his horse. They headed to the TCC stables in silence. Once they were safely back at the entrance, Kevin glanced at Cara. "We never had dessert."

Cara broke her silence with an acknowledging light in her eyes. "We'll have to lie to the chef and tell him it was fabulous."

He dismounted, then reached for her and, once again, she slid down the horse and into his arms. Kevin stared deep into her eyes, holding her loosely around the waist. "It *was* fabulous."

Cara searched his eyes. She had questions, but Kevin had only one answer. He kissed her soundly on the lips, tasting her once again. "Have dinner with me tomorrow night. I'll make up for the dessert we missed."

"How can you do that? I'm sure the chef is on to bigger and better things."

He chuckled, knowing Cara was messing with him. "Easy. I know what you crave."

Cara jammed her hands to her hips and shook her head in denial. "I bet you don't."

"Oh, no? Hot fudge over chocolate cake with vanilla ice cream and a dozen cherries."

"Tasty's?" Cara's smug expression changed to one of longing. "I haven't had Tasty's for—"

"Four and a half years? I took you there for your birthday, remember?"

A thoughtful look crossed her expression and she smiled sadly. "Yeah, I do remember."

"So, how about it? Burgers and dessert at Tasty's tomorrow night?"

Cara opened her mouth, then clamped it closed with a quick snap. He could always tell when she waged a war of decision in her mind.

"Don't overthink it, babe. Just go with it."

The comment opened her eyes wide and she made a quick decision. "Okay. But, Kevin," she began in a solemn tone, "maybe we shouldn't get in over our heads. We both know why I came to Somerset."

"Oh, don't worry. I haven't forgotten."

"G-good."

"But I'm not making any promises."

Cara's mouth tightened into a frown.

Kevin planted a brief kiss over her down-turned lips. "Come on, I'll drive you back to the hotel. You can think about Tasty's all the way home."

* * *

Cara didn't think about Tasty's all the way back to her hotel. She thought about Kevin. He'd touched her in ways she hadn't allowed another man since they'd split up. Sensual images flashed vividly in her head. Her body still prickled. Nope, no man since had even made her feel like trying. Oh, she'd dated at times, but nothing had ever come of it.

Kevin had been sweet and attentive all night and just minutes ago he'd nearly made her forget her own name.

It's Cara Pettigrew, she thought sourly. Not Cara Pettigrew-Novak.

She was still his wife, but in name only. She had stopped being a Novak four years ago.

Cara slipped out of her riding clothes, tugging off the new leather boots Kevin had given her. He'd remembered her shoe size, she realized. How many men would even know their wife's shoe size?

"Remember why you left him," Cara whispered in the quiet of her room. He'd been fun and loving for the first few months of their marriage and then he'd become obsessive and driven. For success? For money? For power? Cara wasn't sure of his motivation, since he'd made a decent living and she'd never complained. She hadn't asked for riches. She'd grown up wealthy. She'd seen how her own father had been driven and how much his obsession had hurt his marriage—and her. She'd been the daughter her father never had time for.

"Money doesn't guarantee happiness," she'd tell

Kevin. But her husband hadn't listened. His competitive nature made him want to prove his worth to Cara and her family. He wanted to measure up, she presumed, though she'd never once implied that he wasn't enough for her.

When the hotel phone rang, Cara was grateful for the interruption of her thoughts.

"Oh, hi, Mom."

Perhaps *grateful* was too strong a word. Her mom had been like a watchdog lately and she was the last person Cara wanted to speak with about Kevin. Especially after what had happened between them tonight. Ever since Cara had made her decision to divorce Kevin, her mother had been *overly* supportive.

"Did he sign the papers yet?"

Cara flinched. Her mother got right to the point. She couldn't possibly tell her mother the truth, that she'd been blackmailed into sleeping with her estranged husband before he'd sign on the dotted line. "No, Mom. Not yet. But we had a…meeting tonight. Kevin is cooperating."

"But, dear, I don't see why there's a problem. You're not asking for much. Actually, you're being quite fair with the settlement. What's the holdup?"

What was the holdup? She didn't know what purpose it served to hang around Somerset for two weeks, but she had to tell her mother something. "Well, Kevin is really busy."

"He hasn't changed," her mother chimed in bitterly. "Just like your father."

Cara swallowed that and continued, "Mom, you know I liked living in Somerset. I'm catching up with friends while I'm here. Taking a little vacation."

"Dear, a vacation is relaxing in a villa in Siena, not begging for signed divorce papers from your husband. I'm worried about you, Cara. You've done so well for yourself in Dallas."

"I was happy here, too, once upon a time."

Her mother's silence was quite telling. She couldn't blame her for being protective. Cara had been hurt by the separation. She'd really loved Kevin, and no mother wants to see her child in pain. Cara understood all that.

"I know, dear, that's why ending it quickly is better for you. It's been dragged out long enough."

"I agree with you, Mom. And I'll get back to Dallas as soon as I can."

"Well, all right. I hope to see you home soon. I love you, dear."

"Love you, too."

Cara hung up the phone and took a long pull of oxygen, thankful the conversation hadn't lasted too long.

When the phone rang again, Cara let it ring four times. She was through talking for the day. All she wanted to do was climb into bed and get to sleep.

But her curiosity got the better of her. She picked

up the receiver, hoping it wasn't her mother on the other end with more pearls of wisdom.

"Hello?"

"Hi, baby." The deep timbre of Kevin's voice oozed through the phone line. "What are you doing?"

"I'm getting out of my…uh, getting ready for bed."

"Yeah? Me, too. I just got out of the shower."

The visual image of Kevin's hard-ripped body wet from head to toe and wrapped in a skimpy towel swept through her mind. She mouthed a silent *oh*, thankful that the word didn't slip out accidentally.

She cleared her throat.

"What do you wear to bed these days?" Kevin asked.

The question was so audacious, Cara laughed. "Wouldn't you like to know?"

"I would, Cara," he said with quiet sincerity.

"Nothing."

Kevin let go a sexy groan.

"Much. Nothing much. I mean, just an old Dancing Lights T-shirt."

"I can picture you wearing that."

"Kevin, why are you calling so late?"

"Had a good time tonight, Cara. Just wanted you to know."

Cara nibbled on her lower lip. She squeezed her eyes shut, yet couldn't shake off images from tonight of Kevin's lips on hers, his mouth making love to her breasts, the tantalizing look of pure lust in his deep-blue eyes when he'd taken off her blouse. "Thank you." She paused, then added, "It was a good night. I enjoyed riding Dream Catcher."

"I thought you might."

"Why are you being so sweet to me?" Cara blurted. She couldn't figure out his motivation. "Our marriage is ending."

Kevin didn't miss a beat. "Yes, but there's no reason we can't be friends, Cara. No reason we can't end this on a happy note."

"Marriages usually don't end on happy notes, sweetheart."

He paused, and she realized she'd used his favorite endearment. "Ours could. We can be different from everyone else. So, are you picturing me dripping wet in my towel or what?"

Cara gasped and then laughed aloud. He'd caught her, but she'd rather die than admit it. "I see you haven't lost your sense of humor after all, Kevin."

"I've lost a lot of things, Cara." His playful mood suddenly changed. "But not my sense of humor."

Cara didn't want to deal with the serious tone of his voice now. Sudden panic developed and she searched for an escape. "Kevin, I'd better get to bed."

"Yeah, me, too. Sleep tight, babe. Dream good dreams."

Cara nearly choked out a quick good-night. She knew what would fill her dreams tonight.

Good or bad, they'd be of Kevin.

Wearing nothing but a small towel.

* * *

The next day the image of Kevin stayed with her all morning long. Restless from those thoughts, Cara left the Four Seasons and walked the Houston streets, stopping in at boutiques along the way— she was bored with the few changes of clothes she'd brought for a trip she had thought would only take two days.

She'd told her mother she'd be taking a little vacation and, though she'd had to rearrange her entire schedule to stay on in Houston, Cara decided, a shopping spree would do her good. Why not enjoy the city while she was here?

By the end of the day, she'd filled two shopping bags with gifts for her dance instructors, a Gucci French flap wallet for her mother and several new outfits for herself, including a scarlet dress to match the new Valentino slingbacks she'd purchased.

The time had flown by. She had just enough time to rush back to the hotel and shower before Kevin came knocking.

It bothered her that she'd changed her clothes three times before her date with him for burgers at Tasty's. Why was she trying to look pretty for Kevin?

But the minute she opened the door and saw the glint of appreciation in his eyes, she thought it was all worth it.

"Wow, you look great. Too good for Tasty's." Kevin toured her body up and down leisurely, and Cara knew a moment of satisfaction.

She'd tried on the dresses she'd picked up today, but decided instead on a pair of formfitting, black pants, very high black heels and a white, flowing, off-the-shoulder blouse belted at the waist with a gold-and-black twist rope. "Stop right there if you think you're gonna weasel your way out of taking me to Tasty's."

"Okay," Kevin said with a teasing twist of his lips. "If I have to. Are you ready to go or do you want to invite me in?"

He peeked over her shoulder and into her hotel room. His gaze focused on her king-size bed. Cara wasn't about to let him in. Her husband was a dangerous man and she'd never been able to resist him when he smiled and spoke with charm.

Kevin still had a perfect body, broad of shoulder and slightly muscular, enough to show his strength without overkill. Four years hadn't changed that. His grooming was impeccable, and darn if he didn't look like he belonged on the cover of *GQ*.

Right now, his blue eyes gleamed with the kind of mischief that could get them both into deep trouble. She shoved at his chest lightly and pushed him out the door. "I'm ready for a burger."

Kevin took her hand from his chest and entwined their fingers. He leaned over to whisper in her ear. "And I'm ready for dessert. It's been a long time, Cara. I need to satisfy my craving."

Four

Kevin helped Cara into his jet-black Jaguar, and then got in and started the engine. His Jag roared to life. All that power at his fingertips at one time had been a big turn-on. But now, Kevin looked across the seat to find his wife sitting beside him and he couldn't think of a bigger turn-on. Cara, dressed for a casual date with him in her classy style, took his breath away.

He gritted his teeth with determination. He wasn't going to make it easy for her to walk away from their marriage. Damn her, anyway. She'd been the primary reason he'd worked sixteen hours a day. She'd come from wealth, and his pride wouldn't allow her to climb down that ladder to marry someone who couldn't provide her the same sort of elevated life-style.

The success he'd achieved had been for her and for their marriage. But her patience had run out and she'd followed suit. He'd never forgive her for leaving him high and dry. The humiliation he'd suffered alone was reason enough for this retaliation. But it was more than that. He'd loved Cara. Really loved her. And she'd destroyed that love.

Cara glanced his way with a quizzical look. "You're quiet."

"It's been a long day."

Kevin snapped on the CD player and smiled. "Oldies, to get us in the mood."

Elvis came on and Cara turned up the volume to "All Shook Up." She knew all the words and sang along with the music. Her toes tapped in rhythm and she swayed her body back and forth. Graceful and elegant, Cara knew how to move.

He'd been resentful when he'd learned about her success with Dancing Lights, somehow seeing the studio as his competition. She'd moved from him to bigger things. Yet, from a purely professional stand-point, he secretly admired her acumen. She hadn't used her family's money for the start-up of her enterprise, but instead had taken out small-business bank loans to fund the studios. Now she was willing to end their marriage to expand her business.

Kevin pushed those bitter thoughts out of his mind. He was on a mission and couldn't forget his game plan.

By the time they reached Tasty's, his spirits had lifted and he grabbed Cara's hand as they bounded up the steps to the fifties diner. They sat in a red-vinyl corner booth and ordered cherry Cokes and Tasty Burgers.

The dated chrome jukebox stood in the opposite corner next to the long Formica lunch counter, and mini-jukeboxes anchored each booth. "Pick some songs," Kevin said as he put two quarters in.

They both leaned in close to view the playlist. "Oh, look. They have one-hit wonders! 'Pretty Little Angel Eyes' was one of my favorites." Cara punched in its number, along with a few other obscure songs from the past.

"What do you suppose happened to these artists?" she asked, her expression thoughtful.

He shrugged. "They tried and failed. They probably went on to lead productive lives in some other field."

Cara nodded. "One would hope. It'd be a shame not to do what you love to do, though."

"Most people don't, Cara. Most don't enjoy the work they do. They simply have to do it to survive."

Cara's sky-blue eyes softened. "I feel extremely lucky that I found something I love to do."

Kevin searched her expression for any sign of regret and found none. It irked him that she could dismiss their marriage so easily. "You were always good at everything you attempted."

"Thank you," she said. She sent him a smile that flattened quickly.

"What's wrong?" Kevin asked, curious about her change of expression.

She shook her head and looked down at the tabletop. "Nothing."

"Something," he prodded.

She lifted her shoulders. "It's just that, at times, I think I failed as…a wife."

Floored by her admission, Kevin furrowed his brow. "Why?"

Emotions surfaced on her face and her eyes narrowed with pain. "I don't know. Maybe because nothing I said or did kept you at home."

Kevin leaned way back in his seat and studied her.

She continued. "My mother had the same issue with my dad. He was never home. Always working, until the day he died. You know he died of a heart attack. Fell facedown on his desk at the office." Cara looked up for a second, holding back tears. "My mother said he died doing what he loved best."

Anger bubbled in his gut. Cara had it all wrong if she was comparing her father to him. Their situations were entirely different. Cara's father had had more wealth than he knew what to do with, while Kevin had had nothing and worked hard to bring their life up to a certain standard of living. He'd been determined to make his first million by age twenty-five.

For Cara.

Always for Cara.

"You think I didn't love you enough?" Kevin asked. "That I wasn't home because I wasn't…

what? Happy with you? Or because I found you lacking in some way?"

Cara shrugged. "It doesn't matter now, Kevin."

They'd had this argument before, but never with so much raw honesty. "I say it does—"

"Hey, Novak." Lance walked in with Darius and both strode to their table. Kevin winced. He needed them here like a hole in the head.

Lance ignored Kevin and nearly lifted Cara out of her seat to give her a bear hug. "My God, you look great! It's good to see you, Cara."

"Same here, Lance."

Darius moved in and gave Cara a hug, too, his low, easy voice greeting her. "You have brightened my day, woman."

"Hi, Darius. How have you been?"

"I've got no complaints."

Cara beamed seeing the two and, without invitation, both Lance and Darius took a seat, cramming Cara and Kevin into the booth. Kevin sat back and listened as Cara and his friends caught up on their lives.

The interruption actually was more beneficial than he'd originally thought, since it had lifted Cara's mood. They'd gotten way off course with the discussion earlier and Kevin fully intended on charming his wife tonight. He'd been thinking about seeing her all day. And if nothing else, he could rely on a sinfully erotic chocolate dessert to get her in a risky frame of mind.

* * *

Cara had indulged herself fully, devouring obscene, hot-fudge cake while enjoying Kevin and his friends. She'd missed their friendship and remembered how much fun they'd all had in college. At the time, Kevin was the only one of the three men in a serious relationship. Now, the opposite was true. Lance had Kate, and Darius had Summer, while she and Kevin teetered on the edge of a divorce.

"They haven't changed much." Cara smiled, feeling melancholy on the drive back to her hotel.

"Those clowns? They'll never change." Kevin grinned.

When he stopped at a red light, he glanced at her, then leaned over to wipe a smudge of hot fudge from her bottom lip. "You're messy."

"Am not."

Kevin licked the hot fudge from his thumb, making Cara squirm a little in her seat. His gaze focused on her mouth, and erotic thoughts entered her head.

"Oh, no?" Kevin's voice went low and deep. "Then why do I have to clean you up?"

Puzzled, Cara squinted. "You don't have to—"

"Yeah, I do." He leaned in farther to cup her head in his hand and slanted his mouth over hers, his tongue doing a thorough swipe over her lips. Cara relished the liberties he took with her, enjoying every second of the kiss. When she began to kiss him back, savoring the moment, the car behind them honked.

"Darn it," Kevin said, moving away. He glanced

in the rearview mirror at the car behind them. "Hold your horses, buddy." Kevin straightened in his seat and drove out of the intersection.

Cara's chuckle had him turning her way.

"What's so funny?"

"You haven't changed your driving habits. Still arguing with everyone on the road."

His eyes twinkled. "Idiots. All of them." When he looked at Cara, a deep, rumbling laugh emerged.

"All of them but you, right?"

"You got that right, babe." His charming grin unnerved her.

Cara settled in her seat, still smoldering from that one red-light kiss and feeling light of heart at the same time. Kevin and chocolate had that effect on her.

Memories flooded her senses of all the silly, light-hearted moments they had shared during their courtship. Kevin had been entertaining and easy to be with. He'd been irresistible, too, and Cara found that tonight, all those traits that made up the man she'd loved had surfaced.

Kevin reached for her hand. "It's early and a beautiful night. Want to take a walk?"

Cara didn't hesitate. She'd enjoyed the evening and didn't want it to end. "I'd like that."

Kevin squeezed her hand and nodded. "I know just the place."

Cara leaned back in her seat, trusting Kevin to entertain her. He'd been doing a good job of it since she'd arrived back in Houston. Though their marriage was over, this short time together would help them heal from wounds inflicted years earlier. Maybe this was the salve they needed to repair their injuries so they could move on with their lives.

Whatever the reason for her carefree mood, Cara wouldn't analyze it too deeply. She was on vacation from life at the moment, a small black hole in time where she and her soon-to-be-ex husband could enjoy each other's company without repercussions.

She'd forget his blackmail for the time being, shoving his motives out of her head. In less than two weeks she'd be back in Dallas, planning her new studio design, doing what she loved doing.

Kevin stopped the car on a dirt road that overlooked Somerset Lake. Brilliant moonlit waters glistened with sapphire illumination. Kevin got out of the car and opened the door for her.

The air felt heavy and warm, typical for a summer Texas night. Crickets chirped on and off and, in the space of quiet, the gentlest rippling of waves could be heard.

Cara swallowed hard as she took in the view. This was the place they'd come with all their friends, to have picnics and bonfires during the summer. This was *their* place, the spot right beyond the picnic tables, where she and Kevin had first admitted their love for one another.

Cara took Kevin's offered hand and followed him down a dusky, bluebonnet-laden path that led to the water. She took each step with care. She hated trampling on the flowers.

"You're not going to hurt them, babe. They look delicate, but they're resilient."

Cara had heard that from Kevin before, in much the same way, but not about bluebonnets. He'd spoken those words about her when they'd had arguments about his workaholic tendencies.

You look delicate, but I know you're resilient.

Apparently, he hadn't thought she could be hurt. Yet even the most durable of flowers had a breaking point.

"Why take the chance?" she said softly. When Kevin glanced at her, she shrugged. "I don't want to destroy them."

Kevin let the comment go and Cara doubted he caught her true meaning.

"Remember this place?" he asked.

"How could I not? We came here almost every weekend in the summer."

"That was some summer, wasn't it?"

She knew he meant the summer when they'd fallen in love. They'd been inseparable. She nodded slowly and held his hand as they walked along the lakeshore.

"Tell me what happened after you left Somerset."

Cara took a long, slow breath. A cricket chirped a few times, before she was able to formulate the words. "I… It was hard, Kevin. The hardest time of my life."

Kevin remained silent. He gazed ahead, refusing to look into her eyes.

"When I decided to start Dancing Lights, my whole world opened up again."

Kevin's mouth twisted, though he tried very hard to conceal his angst.

Cara didn't want to spoil the evening by talking about a sore subject. "I'm sorry, but you asked."

They walked along the little cove and reached a clearing by another group of redwood picnic benches.

"Care to show me a thing or two about dancing? You know I have two left feet."

"Here? There's no music. And you *don't* have two left feet. As I recall, you have some pretty good moves."

Kevin grinned with mischief. He clamped his hands on her waist and pulled her against him. "As *I* recall, you liked all my moves."

Cara gasped, immersed in the gleam of his dark blue eyes.

"But I'm talking about dance moves, babe. I could use a refresher, since I'm inviting you to Lance and Kate's wedding reception at the club. I wouldn't want to embarrass you with my lackluster dance steps."

Cara blinked in surprise. She couldn't go to Lance's reception with Kevin. It was one thing to see him for a few casual dates privately, but being on his arm at a formal affair would give the wrong impression and make her dream things she had no right dreaming. "You won't have to. I can't go."

"How do you know? I haven't told you the date yet."

"Because," Cara said, stepping away from him to look at the calm waters for comfort. Weddings always made her sentimental and she already had enough to deal with. She didn't need a reminder of their utter failure. "It's just that I think—"

"Shh, you think too much," Kevin said softly, searching her eyes. "You're so beautiful in moonlight, Cara." He leaned in and kissed her tenderly on the lips.

Her insides melted at his gentle touch and she reached up on tiptoes to kiss him back, wrapping her arms around his neck. Maybe it was this place and the memories it evoked, or maybe she'd just been too long without any real tenderness in her life, but right now, she needed to be with Kevin, kissing him and feeling like a woman again.

It wasn't long before Kevin's kisses turned her into Silly Putty, except there was nothing silly about the intensity he displayed. He pulled her along, walking backward until he sat upon the edge of a picnic table. He fitted her between his legs and continued to nibble on her mouth until he drew his lips downward to the base of her throat.

Pinpricks of excitement flew up and down her body. She tingled everywhere, breathing in his sexy cologne. The musky scent she recognized from years before drove her further into oblivion.

It was easy for him to untie her rope belt and pull her blouse down. With a groan of appreciation, he murmured her name and her heart rate sped up.

Kevin unfastened her bra with adept fingers and he pulled the garment away from her. "Damn it, sweetheart," he murmured, the curse a soft and beautiful endearment.

Exposed from the waist up, the pushed-down sleeves of her blouse trapping her arms slightly, Cara could only watch as Kevin touched her breasts, caressing, weighing, cupping her with such tenderness, she wanted to cry.

He made eye contact as he flicked his thumbs over her nipples, toying with them and making her moan with pleasure.

"You still like me touching you," he whispered, his torturous fingers breaking her out in a sweat.

She bit her lip and nodded. She *loved* the way Kevin touched her. He'd been the only man who could turn her on so fast, so furiously. But Cara gave as good as she got and she never let Kevin have the last word. "Seems to me," she said, breathless, "you could put that mouth to better use."

Kevin chuckled, then clamped his hands around her trapped arms and brought her closer. Her breast grazed his mouth and he teased her with tiny tongue swipes until her knees nearly buckled.

"Better?" he asked in a whisper and she nodded enthusiastically.

He filled his mouth with her, suckling and blowing hot breath over her breast. Her nipple stood erect and a rush of sizzling heat invaded her body. Everything below her waist throbbed.

Kevin was in no better shape. His body was rigid, the bulge of his desire pressed against her clothes. Crazy thoughts entered her head of making love to Kevin right here, out in the open, beside the lake where they'd first revealed their love for each other.

Kevin's thoughts couldn't have been far behind. He kissed her soundly and stood up, his manhood grazing her between the legs. "I need more, baby."

Cara nodded and helped Kevin unzip her pants. He cosseted her close and slipped his hand inside. With nimble fingers, he pulled her panties aside and cupped her womanhood.

"Ohh." His touch sent her mind reeling. She'd been so long without this, without Kevin bringing her pleasure.

Alone at the lake in the darkness, the night lit only by moonlight, Cara succumbed to Kevin's ministrations. He slid his hand back and forth, his fingertips caressing her most sensitive skin. She rocked and swayed, and he kissed her while she moved over his hand.

"You feel so good, Cara," he whispered over her lips. He slipped one finger inside.

Cara's eyes closed. She surrendered to Kevin's will. Every single part of her body tingled as he stroked her, slipping his finger up and down until she moved in rhythm like the music of a sexy samba. When she arched her back, Kevin followed her, sliding his lips along her throat, creating sensations that burned like a branding iron.

Whimpers of pleasure tumbled from her lips and Cara's face twisted in ecstasy. "Oh, sweet heaven."

Kevin cupped her breast with one hand and stroked her unmercifully with the other. Again and again, until Cara's body rocked out of control.

"It's so good, baby. Remember?"

Cara remembered. Kevin had always been an unselfish lover. But her thoughts stopped there, because she was too far gone to answer him. Her pleasure heightened and heightened, Kevin drawing out every quiver, every earth-shattering morsel of ecstasy, relentless in his pursuit.

Her muscles contracted and squeezed, her body quaked, and Kevin stopped his assault, allowing her to enjoy this moment on her own terms. He knew, oh, yes, how he knew to bring her the utmost pleasure.

Her orgasm came in slow, torturous, drawn-out bursts. Cara relished each mind-blowing second of shuddering release. Then slowly, slowly she came back down to earth.

When she opened her eyes, Kevin was watching her, his gaze smoldering with lust. "That was—"

"Heaven," Cara whispered, not shy about her display.

Kevin shook his head. "The sexiest thing I've ever witnessed."

Cara glanced down at his obvious erection. "Are you…okay?"

"I could make love to you ten times on this picnic table and not be satisfied."

Cara squirmed, tempted by the erotic thought.

Kevin worked her zipper up and handed her back her bra. "But a deal's a deal."

Fully sated and feeling very lighthearted, Cara dressed. "A man of his word."

Kevin inhaled a sharp breath. She knew how much he'd held back, for her pleasure. "Would have been safer to teach me how to dance."

Cara couldn't contain her smile. "Safety is over-rated at times."

Five

"So, you'll come to Lance and Kate's reception with me?"

Cara turned to Kevin before entering her hotel room. He stood close, boxing her in by the door. Her face still glowed from the attention he'd paid to her at the lake, and the taste of her lips still lingered on his mouth.

"Are you trying to manipulate me?" she asked coyly.

Kevin winced and faked a stab wound to the heart. "You're killing me, Cara."

Cara nibbled on her lower lip with indecision. She'd had him at his boiling point. It had been all he could do not to make love to her on that picnic table tonight. Desire and lust combined made for a heavy aphrodisiac.

"Why do you want me to go?"

Kevin tilted his head and spoke in a serious tone. "Regardless of what has happened between us, Lance has always been your friend. I know he'd want you to be there."

"Why do you?" Cara asked, searching his eyes.

"You're awfully suspicious."

"Don't I have a right to be? After all, you're blackmailing me."

"It's not blackmail, Cara. We made a deal. And tonight, I asked you to celebrate the marriage of a good friend. It's as simple as that."

Kevin wanted her on his arm that night and he wanted to spend as much time with her as possible during these two weeks, but it surprised him how much it mattered to him.

Cara finally relented. "Okay. I'll go and share in the celebration. Lance is a good man."

Kevin nodded, glad that she'd changed her mind. "Good night, Cara." He leaned in and pressed his mouth to hers, relishing the soft, subtle nuances of her giving lips and baby-soft skin. "I had a good time tonight."

Cara closed her eyes briefly. An image of her panting out a rocking orgasm flashed in his head.

"Uh, Kevin. Maybe we shouldn't—"

Kevin leaned in and kissed her a second time, stopping her next thought. "I'll call you tomorrow."

She gazed into his eyes and shook her head as if

trying to figure him out before turning to enter her hotel room.

Kevin left her and drove to his penthouse. He stripped out of his clothes immediately and walked into an icy-cold shower. The brisk spray rained down, easing his stubborn lust. But sexy images of Cara stayed with him throughout. It wasn't easy to wash Cara from his system.

He wanted to make her pay for abandoning him. He wanted to charm her and bend her to his will. He'd succeeded somewhat, but Cara had always been bright. She was correct to be suspicious of him. The only trouble was that he, too, paid a price for his little plan.

He wanted her.

After he toweled off, he headed for his bar and poured himself two fingers of bourbon. Leaning against the black-granite counter, he lifted his glass in midair. "Here's to you, Cara. My wife for just a few more days."

After her lake encounter with Kevin, Cara warned herself she was playing with fire and vowed to keep her distance from her husband until Lance and Kate's reception. It was much safer that way. She needed to keep her perspective and remember why she'd come to Houston.

She'd maintained that resolve for exactly twelve hours, until Kevin knocked at her door midmorning, wearing a full Astros baseball getup. She glanced at him, puzzled, noting his red jersey and baseball cap with the Astros' official star logo. He waved box-seat tickets for the afternoon game in front of her and shot her a delicious grin.

When it dawned on her what he had in mind, she could hardly refuse his enticing offer. She was a huge Houston fan, going back to her high-school days. Going to a day game felt sinful and luxurious, and she felt that doubly with Kevin by her side.

Now, she sat in a box seat at Minute Maid Park, just behind home plate, eating a hot dog and slurping down a Diet Coke.

"Want another?" he asked, after inhaling two hot dogs in record time.

"Nope, but toss me that bag of peanuts and I'm good to go."

Kevin smiled and set the bag on her lap. "Have at it, babe."

They munched on peanuts, booed the bad calls, cheered the good ones and jumped from their seats when an Astro player made it on base. Kevin excused himself for a minute and when he returned, he plopped a red cap with a big white star on her head and handed her a jersey that matched his.

"Thank you!" After she put the jersey on over her blouse, she reached over and planted a big kiss on his cheek.

Kevin turned his head toward her and her kiss slid to his lips. He tasted of mustard and soda and sunshine and their kiss lasted far longer than expected. Kevin took her into his arms and, much like two teenagers in love, they lost themselves.

"Hey, get a room!"

The shout came from a few rows back and Kevin smiled as he broke off the kiss. "Not a bad idea."

"Oh!" Cara straightened in her seat, a full flush of heat rising up her neck. She refused to look Kevin's way for a few minutes but she did hear him chuckle several times.

The Astros won the game and, with their spirits buoyed, they strolled the ballpark hand-in-hand until the crowds diminished. Cara stood in the Grand Union lobby, the famous entrance to the ballpark that went back to the early beginnings of Houston. "Remember when they built the stadium?"

"Yeah, traffic was stopped up for months."

Cara glanced at him. "But you thought it was cool that they'd use Union Station as the entrance."

"Still do. It brings a lot of people to the downtown area. From a business standpoint, it was a great idea."

"Speaking of business, how did you manage to get away from the office today?"

When they were living as man and wife, Kevin would have rather cut off his right arm than take a day off from work.

"I'll make up for it tonight. Got a load of paperwork to sift through."

Cara figured as much. He'd never let his work go, not even for a day. There were times he wouldn't come to bed until two, the computer more of an enticement than she was. In the morning, she'd wake up to find him gone.

She remembered those lonely days and nights. Those memories stayed with her and marred the pleasant day she'd just had.

She remained quiet as Kevin took her back to the hotel, deciding it was a good idea not to invite him in. "I had fun today. Thank you for the invitation." Her voice stiff and formal, Cara made up for her lack of grace with a little smile.

Kevin didn't seem to notice the change in her. "Me, too. It's been ages since I went to a game."

"Because you're too busy?"

Kevin weighed her question, studying her. "I know how to delegate work now, Cara," he said, his tone none too gracious. "I haven't gone to a game because…hell, you're gonna make me say it?"

Stunned, Cara blinked. "Say what?"

Kevin shook his head and cursed. "Because it's what *we* did. Me and you."

"Oh." She wasn't sure she understood.

"I went a few times with the guys," he admitted. Then Kevin's voice went deep, and he tapped her baseball cap twice, planting it farther down on her forehead. "But they don't look as cute as you in a baseball cap."

Before she could react, Kevin leaned down and kissed her soundly on the lips, putting to shame the kiss they'd shared at the ballpark. After five minutes of making out hot and heavy at her door, Kevin backed away and caught his breath, his eyes devastatingly blue. "I'd better go. I'll call you tomorrow."

Cara slumped by the door, not knowing if she was glad he'd left or angry that, once again, his work took precedence over her.

What difference did it make, anyway?

Soon she'd be the *ex* Mrs. Kevin Novak, and what he did or didn't do with his time wouldn't matter.

She clung to that thought and took it to bed with her, trying not to wonder when Kevin would call her again.

Cara fumed for the next two days. Kevin didn't call. She knew she should be glad that she'd been given a reprieve from the relentless attention he paid her, yet she thought it all a waste of time. He'd forced her to stay in Houston for two weeks to obtain his signature. She'd put her life on hold for him. She'd made umpteen calls to her dance studio, dealing with problems and making important decisions from her hotel room instead of being where she was most needed.

Cara looked in the mirror and fidgeted with her unruly mop of hair, finger-combing strands back in place while she debated about going out for dinner or calling room service. Anger bubbled inside and she decided to take a brisk walk to cool off. She picked up her purse just as the hotel phone rang.

She stared at it for a long while, debating whether to pick up. Finally, she relented. "Hello?" she said, tapping her foot.

"Hi, Cara."

Cara winced when she heard Kevin on the other end. She wished she'd listened to her first instinct and not answered the phone. His voice sounded odd and distant, as if he were calling from a cave. "Where are you?"

"Home. Do you still make that killer chicken soup?"

"My grandma's recipe? Yes, why do you—" Then it dawned on her. Kevin didn't sound like himself. In fact, she'd never heard him sound so *off.* She put two and two together. "Are you sick?"

"You could say that," he whispered.

"How sick?"

"I've been in bed for two days and nights, going crazy."

Guilt washed over her and Cara was ashamed of how many unpleasant thoughts had entered her mind about Kevin. She had been certain that he'd been playing games and toying with her emotions, telling her he'd call and then deliberately avoiding her.

"Do you have a fever?"

"One hundred and two."

Oh, man. She softened immediately. "Have you eaten?"

Certainly a millionaire living in a penthouse would have someone to cook and clean for him.

"Toast, yesterday. Not much of an appetite. But I'm craving your grandmother's soup."

Cara inhaled sharply. She was hardly Kevin's nursemaid, but she was still his wife. And his pride wouldn't allow him to ask, unless he really needed her help. She remembered that Kevin hated being sick, never took a day off to heal and was the worst patient she'd ever seen. "I'll catch a cab and be right over."

"I sent a car for you. You can stop off and get the things you need. He should be there any minute."

Cara sighed. "Kevin, how'd you know I'd come?"

"I didn't," he said, his voice trailing off. Cara backed away from giving him grief—he really sounded ill. "But a man can hope, right?"

Kevin felt better already just knowing Cara was on her way. He didn't know what had hit him since he rarely got sick, but he'd been knocked for a loop after taking Cara to the Astros game. He'd spent the next two days in bed, hating every minute of it. His fever had spiked and he hadn't had a drop of energy. Today, he'd gotten up and worked from his home office until he couldn't move a muscle. He'd climbed back in bed, cursing, and the only thing he'd thought of besides his rotten luck was Cara.

In truth, since she'd come back to town she'd consumed his thoughts. His plan for payback was working exceptionally well. Maybe too well, because he'd spent the past two days dreaming of her and the dusky, molten look he put on her face every time they came together. Building up to their one night of lovemaking was killing him, but he enjoyed every torturous minute.

Tonight, he decided, he'd call a truce. He couldn't

take advantage when she'd come so willingly to help him recover, but he felt no guilt whatsoever for the little fib he'd told to get her here.

His fever had broken before he'd called her and he was feeling human again. But he hadn't lied about his craving. He wanted to see Cara in his kitchen, cooking her grandmother's hearty chicken soup. It was the best way to get her to his penthouse—he doubted she'd have come otherwise. But why the hell he'd pictured Cara in his kitchen in a little domestic scene instead of sprawled out across his silk sheets was a mystery to him.

Kevin took a shower, hoping to wipe out the last remnants of his fever and bring some color back to his face. He soaped up and the cool spray of water raining down invigorated him. He shampooed hair that he'd let go for two days and, once he'd turned the faucet off, he toweled dry and stepped out of the shower. This was the most activity he'd had in two days. Looking in the mirror, he let out a groan. "Shabby, Novak," he muttered, "and pale."

His beard served well to cover his sallow appearance, so he opted not to shave. After slipping on his briefs and a comfortable pair of jeans, he threw on a black shirt but didn't have the energy to button it. When the doorbell chimed, he walked the distance to the front door on legs that still felt like rubber.

He opened the door and found Cara holding a brown sack of groceries. "Hi, Kevin."

Cara's gaze immediately drifted to his bare chest, where his shirt spread open. His heartbeat sped up watching lust invade her pretty blue eyes. The flash of instant desire scorched him more than the fever he'd just fought. Then she blinked and redirected her gaze to his face, the moment gone. Soon, he'd put that look back on her face. Tonight, though, it was all he could muster to take the grocery bag from her arms. "My salvation. I'm glad you came, Cara."

"I, uh, sure. I'll make the soup and then let you rest. You really should be in bed."

"I've *been* in bed. It's boring. And lonely."

Cara arched her brow. "I'll find my way around. Point me toward the kitchen."

He placed his hand on the delicate curve of her back, wondering what she'd been up to today, dressed in a classy, sleeveless black-lace blouse and white slacks. Had he interrupted her plans tonight? "C'mon. I'll show you where it is."

Cara darted glances back and forth from one room to the other. Kevin liked his penthouse, having decorated it himself, but he imagined Cara didn't. Too much black and granite and hard angles for her liking—there was nothing here that spoke to a woman's feminine side.

"It's a nice place," she said politely. "Big. How many rooms?"

"Seven." He shrugged. "It's home for now."

When they reached the kitchen, Kevin set the bag on the polished-granite countertop. Cara took in the state-of-the-art stainless steel appliances and nodded. "Either you don't cook much, or you have an expert cleaning staff."

Kevin cracked a smile and it actually hurt his face. He hadn't smiled in two days. "Both. I know the place looks sterile. I eat out a lot or bring in food. You know I'm not a cook."

"Yeah, I remember. Boiling an egg is your specialty." She smiled wide. "I thought that might have changed."

He sat down on the counter stool across the island from Cara, content to watch her. "Some things have changed, but not my cooking abilities. I'm still pretty hopeless in the kitchen, but I make up for it in other ways."

She blinked, looking a little flustered, and rubbed her hands down her slacks. "Okay, well, I'll just get started."

She removed the groceries from the bag and started laying things out, opening and closing kitchen drawers until she had all the utensils she needed. "Are you going to sit there and watch me?"

He nodded. "Unless you need help."

God, he hoped she didn't. He'd sat down because his rubber legs needed the break. He'd felt better after his shower but, as the hour wore on, weakness consumed him again.

"Nope, this is a one-woman job." She smiled and went to work efficiently. "Just watch and learn."

Cara scooped up the carrots and potatoes she'd cut into small chunks and tossed them into the big soup pot. The chicken pieces were already cooking and she'd used caution with the spices. Normally, she'd spice up the soup to give it a sharp bite, but she had to stick to more bland ingredients for Kevin's sake.

He watched her intently, making small talk, asking her about the recipe, truly engaged in what she was doing. But each time Cara glanced at him, he appeared to slump lower on the stool. His voice droned in quiet tones and only his stubborn nature kept him in the kitchen instead of the bed, where he really needed to be.

"You're exhausted, sweetheart," she said softly. "The soup's going to need an hour of simmering. Let me get you into bed. I'll come get you when it's ready."

Kevin pursed his lips and stared at her with feigned irritation. Hell would freeze over before Kevin would ever admit defeat, but she knew he was grateful for the reprieve. "Only because you called me sweetheart."

"That was my strategy all along," she said, wiping her hands on a dish towel. She moved to his side of the island. "Can you get to your bedroom okay?"

He lowered his dark blond lashes. "Sure, but it'd be more fun if you helped me."

Cara couldn't tell if he was joking. He really did appear weak and his color had faded since she'd first arrived. She feared he'd overdone it. "Okay, I'll get you there."

Kevin stood and wrapped his arm around her shoulder. She followed his lead to the farthest room down the hallway. Double doors opened to a room that could only be described as a suite in itself. A black-manteled fireplace stood across from the massive bed. An enormous flat-screen television covered one wall and a room-size balcony ventured out from two French doors, overlooking the Houston skyline.

Cara refrained from commenting. Kevin had certainly come up in the world. Everything he owned spoke of great wealth. He had achieved his goals. He was a brilliant success. A part of her wanted to shed tears all over again, for the marriage that he'd sacrificed without realizing it. For the love that had taken the brunt of his success and for the shattering of vows spoken.

There was a moment of awkward silence when they'd reached his beautifully crafted bed. Would this be the place where they'd seal their divorce deal next week?

Cara heaved a sigh and ducked away from Kevin. "There you go," she said brightly. "I'd better go stir the soup. Get some rest, okay?"

Kevin removed his shirt and let it drop slowly. He stood by the bed in jeans and bare feet, his short hair disheveled and his face sporting stubble that made him look dangerous and sexy. Dear heaven. Cara's breath caught tight in her throat. Her husband was gorgeous, ripped with lean muscle and extremely appealing even in his weakened state.

She shook her head and backed out of the room. Images of Kevin opening the door earlier with droplets of water beaded on his fine chest hair invaded her thoughts. She'd wanted to lick each one and then run her hands over him, again and again. "Chase those thoughts from your head, Cara," she whispered as she reentered the kitchen. "And don't you dare fall for Kevin Novak again."

Six

Cara stood over the six-burner Viking range and stirred the soup. Every time she made this soup she thought of the sweet nature of her grandmother, who had taught Cara step-by-step how to prepare it. What set this soup apart from all others was the fresh crushed tomatoes she used and the cup of red wine that she put in during the last twenty minutes of cooking. It was her grandmother's secret ingredient and her signature meal.

She hadn't made this soup once since she and Kevin had broken up. But now, images of standing beside Grandma Flo in her kitchen, helping toss in ingredients, came to mind and lingered in a pleasing way. The aroma of oregano, basil, fresh tomatoes and onion drifted throughout the kitchen and brought her back to a happy time in her childhood.

She had Kevin to thank for that. Not that she wanted to see him sick, but she missed cooking for someone else, deriving great satisfaction in it. "There you go," she said, giving the soup one last stir before allowing it to simmer.

Cara looked about the kitchen, wondering what to do next. She'd already cleaned up the mess she'd made chopping up the ingredients. On impulse, she walked to Kevin's room and peeked inside the double doors that she'd left ajar earlier.

He slept.

That was a good sign. What wasn't a good sign was her unexpected physical attraction to him, seeing him sprawled out on the bed, nearly naked but for the jeans he wore. She had an uncanny urge to both nurture him and make crazy love to him.

Quickly, Cara stepped away and mentally scolded herself. "Don't go there," she whispered. Then curiosity got the better of her and she perused the rooms in the penthouse, looking for signs of…what? Another woman? Something that would clue her in as to what he'd done with the past four years of his life.

Sourly she admitted that Kevin wouldn't have been celibate for four years. She wondered how many relationships he'd had. How many women had he brought up here to admire the view?

She entered his office and noticed a soft, buttery-brown sofa, the only piece of furniture that looked welcoming. His mahogany desk was littered with files and papers. She walked behind the desk to look out at the Houston skyline and pictured Kevin twirling around in his chair to take a breather and look out the window. "Nice."

Cara wandered over to a sturdy wall unit and lifted up a few picture frames sitting on the shelf, noting that every scene depicted Kevin with one or more of his friends—Lance and Kevin on the golf course, and Darius, Mitch, Lance and Kevin on the tennis court. She glanced at a photo of Kevin with Kate and Lance, the happy threesome smiling into the camera.

Cara picked up a picture of Kevin standing beside his parents at his University of Texas graduation. Still in cap and gown, Kevin's face displayed confidence and determination. She saw the resolute gleam in his eyes—nothing would stop him from achieving his goals. Had she been so blindsided by love that she hadn't noticed that quality in him before? Or had she thought she wouldn't fall victim to his dogged persistence and drive? Cara had been at his graduation and at one point had stood beside him and his parents for a photo. But that picture, she presumed, was long gone, tossed out when she'd left, which he considered abandonment and she considered survival.

Regret and nostalgia brought a whisper of a sigh to her lips. She recalled how they'd celebrated his graduation that night.

In bed.

And making plans for their future.

Now, she wondered who'd be making future plans with Kevin once he was single again. Bemused, Cara's curiosity escalated. She entered the other two bedrooms in the penthouse and noticed, with a good deal of relief, there were no pictures of Kevin with a woman. She dared to peek inside the walk-in closets, loathing the nosy-body she'd become but too curious to keep herself from snooping.

Cara walked back into the kitchen and stirred the soup again. Thankfully, it was ready. She closed her eyes and the flavorful aroma hit her anew, but she couldn't shake the feeling that she'd learned far more about herself than Kevin on her little escapade through his house.

The elation she felt seeing no signs of another woman anywhere in his home caused her great concern. She nibbled on her lip and made up her mind to get out as quickly as she could.

"Something smells good in here."

Cara whirled around. Kevin stood at the doorway, barefoot in those same soft jeans. Thankfully, as he made his way into the room, he pulled a T-shirt on over his head, covering the chest she itched to touch.

"The soup's ready. I was just about to come get you."

"What, no dinner in bed?" He wiggled his eyebrows in that charming way he had.

"I see you've got your sense of humor back," she bantered. "How're you feeling?"

He stopped his approach to take assessment. "Rested. The best sleep I've had in two days."

"Must be the powers of the soup," she said, taking out a bowl from the dark maple cabinet.

Kevin scratched his head. "The powers of something."

They stared at each other across the kitchen, his deep-blue gaze penetrating her until she thought she'd bubble over, like the soup she'd just prepared.

Cara made herself really busy, slicing French bread she'd bought at a bakery down the street. She poured Kevin a bowl of soup and set a thick slice of bread on his plate.

"I should go," she said.

Kevin's gaze never left hers. He walked over to the cabinet and took down a second bowl. "Do you have a hot date tonight?"

An unfeminine chuckle erupted from her chest. "Yeah, with my book."

"Then stay. Have a bowl of soup with me. I could use the company."

Dumbfounded, Cara watched Kevin's efficient movements around the kitchen. Before she knew it, he'd duplicated his own meal for her.

He took both of the plates to the living room and set them down on a cocktail table. "You'll never guess what's on TV right now."

Cara groaned. She knew Kevin had her. She followed him into the living room. "James Bond marathon."

Kevin worked the remote and Bond's classic opening music played as an image of 007 filled the screen.

"Oh, man, and I really wanted to finish that book tonight."

Kevin smiled and sat down on the sofa, stiff leather squeaking as he got comfortable.

She was a sucker for Bond. They both were. So when Kevin patted the seat directly next to him, Cara didn't hesitate, the temptation too great. She sat down beside him and together they watched the movie and enjoyed her grandmother's delicious, hot soup.

Somewhere between *Dr. No* and *Never Say Never Again,* Kevin felt the grip of illness dissipate. He'd woken up past midnight on his sofa with a more than healthy erection. The flat screen droned in the background, long since forgotten. Cara was sprawled on top of him, her head on his shoulder, her silky blond hair tickling his chin, her soft breathing giving testimony to her slumber.

Kevin let go a silent groan of pain. Cara's breasts crushed his chest, but it was her softly feminine, erotic scent that had his mind reeling with possibilities. For now, all he could do was stroke her hair, weaving tendrils through his fingers. Her blouse had drifted up her back, exposing skin that dipped below the waistband of her white slacks.

Kevin stretched his fingers out, debating whether

to give in to impulse and run his hand over her back and dip under her waistband. Man, oh, man, how he wanted to, but she'd been a good sport about coming over here and making soup so he couldn't very well wake her now for his own selfish reasons.

Could he?

Kevin asked himself, why not? He'd had a reason and purpose to have her stay in Houston for two weeks. She owed him and he meant to make her pay for leaving him high and dry. Having her lying atop him tempted him beyond belief. She'd only be his wife another week, so why not derive as much pleasure as possible from the situation now?

Kevin stroked her back lightly and she stirred, letting go a little moan.

Kevin's erection stiffened. Yet he couldn't bring himself to disturb her peace. Holding her, he closed his eyes again, enjoying the feel of her in his arms. Wouldn't be too long before he'd lose the legal right to do so.

Less than a minute later Cara moved, and Kevin opened his eyes to find her casting him a sleep-hazy look. "Hi, babe."

She blinked, disoriented, and lifted her body somewhat to stare into his eyes. Kevin noted the exact moment when Cara's eyes widened with dawning knowledge of where she was and how aroused she'd made him. "Oh."

"I've recovered," he said, before lifting the corners of his mouth. "But now I have another problem."

Cara pushed against his chest and made a move to get up. "What time is it?"

Kevin wrapped his arms around her, gently bringing her back down. "After midnight."

She looked around the room, spotting a tuxedo-clad Pierce Brosnan racing for his life on the flat screen. "I fell asleep."

"*We* fell asleep."

She stared into his eyes. "How are you?"

"Except for the obvious," he said, his gaze dropping down to her spectacular cleavage, "I'm feeling great."

She stared at him and silence ensued as she took stock of her position and the strain of his jeans against the apex of her legs. "You're turned on."

"Big-time."

She nibbled on her lower lip, clearly panicked. The pulsing sensation where they joined wasn't one-sided. Heat and pressure built and Cara couldn't deny she was just as turned on. "I should go."

"Stay, Cara." Kevin put his hand behind her neck and pulled her head down. They looked into each other's eyes before Kevin nipped at her lips. Once, twice, then he wrapped his arms around her more tightly and those nibbles became full-fledged, hot, hungry kisses.

Cara whimpered in her throat, eager for more and fully aroused. Kevin dipped his tongue into her mouth and swept through, tasting her with long, openmouthed motions. As the kisses went deeper, she moved on him, rubbing her body over his erection until he thought he'd die of agony.

Kevin lifted her enough to bring his mouth to her breast. He suckled her through the lace of her blouse, moistening her until the material became nearly sheer. Her nipple strained, tight. Kevin flicked the tip with his thumb and simultaneously, they both pulled her blouse up and over her head. Kevin didn't take time to undo her bra, he simply reached inside and released her breasts from their enclosure.

Cara kissed him hard on the lips and allowed him free rein to do whatever he wanted. He took his time, cupping, weighing, adoring each breast, licking the tips and wetting each perfect globe until Cara's breathing became frenzied.

She lifted up partway and pushed his T-shirt off over his head. She dropped her mouth on him immediately, kissing his chest, her hands roaming freely. "Ah, Cara," he murmured, his pleasure heightening.

She circled his flat nipples and nipped at the tips, her fingers weaving into his scattered chest hair. She pulled at him and he smiled at her prowess, while his erection strained even harder against his jeans.

He ran his hands in her hair, enjoying every second Cara made love to him. It was better than he remembered, having her hands caress him, having her mouth drive him crazy.

Revenge can be sweet, he thought, and wondered if his plan was working, or if Cara simply derived sexual pleasure from him. Either way, he wouldn't question it now.

Kevin took Cara's hand and set it on his waistband, directly over the zipper that was ready to combust. "Touch me," he whispered. "Like you used to."

Cara closed her eyes and inhaled sharply. Then, after a second of thought, she slid slightly to the side to unsnap his jeans. Kevin held his breath. He ached for her touch, for Cara to ease his need. The top of his waistband opened and, with two nimble fingers, she moved the zipper down slowly.

Cool air hit him yet his body flamed. Her touch was light and tentative as she stroked him initially. He lifted up, slanting his lips over hers, deepening their mounting desire.

"This is dangerous," she whispered between kisses.

"You've never shied away from danger, babe."

"It's better to be safe."

"Didn't you once say safety is overrated?"

Cara laughed and the sound of her lightheartedness turned the tide. Kevin laughed, too, his body no less hard-pressed for her, but they'd reached a playful plateau that they might have called their trademark, once upon a time.

"We always had fun together," he added.

"I know, but I didn't come here for fun."

"Why did you come?"

"Soup, remember?"

"No, I don't remember. Anything that happened more than ten minutes ago is a complete blur."

Cara punched him lightly on the shoulder and Kevin reacted by taking hold of her arm and tugging her down. He tasted her lips again and again, the playfulness forgotten as heat and passion consumed them again.

Kevin relished every second Cara touched him, her soft hand against his shaft stroking him in her subtle then bold ways, creating sizzling hot tension. He wanted nothing more than to ease his lust inside her. To feel her soft perfect body welcome him. Man, oh, man, he remembered how it was to be with Cara. He'd never forgotten. No woman had ever compared. But he couldn't make love to her tonight. Not yet. Kevin sat up abruptly before he lost all control.

"Are you feeling weak again?" she asked, seriously concerned.

"Just a dose of Cara fever," he said with a quick smile.

Her expression softened and Kevin rose before he gave in to his desire to make love to her.

He reached down to grab her hand. "It's late. I'll drive you home."

They dressed quickly, both silent in their thoughts. But when he escorted Cara to her hotel room, she turned to him, puzzled. "Kevin, I don't understand any of this."

She looked sex tousled and beautifully confused. "That makes two of us."

The trouble was, Kevin knew his plan the way a general knew his battle strategy, but that didn't make it any less confusing to him, either. They stared at each other for a long moment, searching one another for the truth and coming up short.

"Thanks for coming to my rescue tonight," he said finally. "The soup was great." Then he added, "You haven't lost your touch."

Kevin turned from Cara and forced himself to walk away without looking back.

Cara was at her wit's end, wanting Kevin so terribly that the tension caused her a sleepless night. Sensibly, she knew she and Kevin were doomed as a couple, so making love to him could only hurt her. Her rational side understood that. But her heart and her body were a different matter. She wanted to have sex with her husband—was that so wrong? She had asked that of herself last night and then again this morning. She craved Kevin. He knew how to make her skin prickle and how to satisfy her innermost desires. But the sad fact remained that, once she got what she wanted, their marriage would be over.

When her cell phone rang, Cara looked at the number and hesitated before answering. "Hi, Kevin."

"You cured me last night."

"I'm...glad."

"How about letting me make it up to you. Dinner, tomorrow night? I promise to be better company. I'll even shave."

Cara laughed. She rubbed the slight beard-burns on her face where his stubble had bruised her last night. Memories rushed forth. She shook her head and knew she should make up an excuse and refuse him.

It's for the best, Cara.

Cara opened her mouth to say no, and surprised herself. "I'd love to."

She slammed her eyes shut. Why did she find Kevin so irresistible? Had he changed? Could she trust him? None of it mattered, anyway. In less than a week she'd be gone, with her signed divorce papers in hand.

After making arrangements with him, she hung up the phone, at odds with herself. When her cell phone rang a second time, she answered it quickly, happy to receive Alicia's call.

"Hi, Cara. It's Alicia."

"Alicia, I'm so glad you called."

"Are we still on for lunch and shopping this afternoon?"

"I'm looking forward to it." Cara needed a girl's day out to clear her mind.

"I'm in town, so I'll pick you up and we'll head to Somerset. Can you be ready in half an hour?"

"Yes." So ready, she thought. "I'll be waiting for you downstairs."

After she hung up the phone, Cara dressed in brown slacks and a sleeveless crème top. She slipped her feet into comfy, chocolate-brown Jimmy Choos and pulled her curly hair back into a tortoiseshell clip. She grabbed her matching handbag and exited the hotel room.

Alicia drove up just as Cara exited the Four Seasons. The doorman wished her a good day and off she went, ready to put Kevin out of her mind for the next few hours.

Cara took in the sights as the bustling downtown soon gave way to quiet residential roads. Somerset, in the heart of Maverick County, was a small, beautifully constructed town northeast of Houston. Cara had once loved living there in a modest home with Kevin. There were times in Dallas when she would be reminded of their house—she'd see a fabric similar in design to her kitchen curtains or smell fresh mint and recall the stone pathway that led to their front door, laden with the herb. She would sigh, wondering how her life had changed so much. Sentimental feelings would rush in, but Cara had always quickly shooed them away.

Now, as Alicia drove on, Cara looked to a digital sign set atop a tall post just outside the front gates of Maverick High School, announcing in flashing yellow letters the first dance of the new semester. "I hear those Friday-night dances were something wild. Lance and Mitch were always going on and on about them. I bet they stopped just short of telling me how much trouble they'd really gotten into back then."

Alicia shrugged. "I wouldn't know. I didn't go to many dances."

"No?"

With a shake of her head, Alicia replied, "No, I, uh, didn't care to…"

"Dance? Now, Alicia, I bet you can move."

"I like to dance," Alicia said carefully, "but Alex

didn't want me to go to the dances. He, uh, thought people looked down on us." Alicia turned to her, her dark eyes almost apologetic. "Alex has a lot of pride."

Cara remembered how protective Alejandro Montoya was of his little sister, just from bits and pieces she'd heard of Kevin's conversations with his friends. Alicia was timid and Alex had done his best to shield her. Cara still couldn't believe that Alex would have had anything to do with the fire at Brody Oil, though he may have been resentful of the men who had more than he had while growing up. He had come from a different social standing, working at the Texas Cattleman's Club as the groundskeeper, but now he was just as wealthy and powerful as Kevin and his friends. Alex may hate the Brodys, but Cara refused to believe he was a criminal.

"You two are very close."

"Yes, and I have to keep reminding him, I'm all grown up now."

"Sometimes men can't see what's right in front of them," Cara acknowledged.

Alicia beamed with amusement. "So true."

They dined at a little outdoor restaurant on Somerset's main street. Wrought-iron chairs and umbrella-covered mosaic-stone tables gave a Spanish ambiance. After glancing at the menu, Cara noted the fare was mostly Southwestern, which suited her just fine. She was in the mood for hometown spice.

She loved eating outdoors on warm days and

didn't get too much chance to do so in Dallas. Usually, she ate her lunch in the office at the dance studio, going over accounts or viewing video of her students' progress.

"This is really nice," Cara said.

"It's new. I thought you might like it."

They sat in silence for a minute looking at the menu and when the waiter walked up, offering the daily specials, Cara and Alicia both decided on spicy Southwestern chicken salad with chipotle, and strawberry margaritas.

The margaritas arrived first. Cara lifted her glass in a toast. "To friends," she said with a smile.

"To friends," Alicia repeated, and they touched together their full margarita glasses before taking a sip.

Cara told Alicia all about her dance studios, explaining about how her background in gymnastics and dance had given her the idea when she and Kevin had split up. She admitted she'd had to do something with her life. She'd been brokenhearted and depressed. Pouring herself into her work and seeing the progress she'd made in just a few short years had come to mean so much to her.

"And now I'm back for a short time."

Alicia cast her a curious look. Cara had never really explained why she'd come back and Alicia had been too polite to inquire, but she assumed her friend was puzzled. If the roles were reversed, Cara would be, too. "I've been spending some time with Kevin."

She couldn't bring herself to confess that the reason she'd been seeing Kevin was his blackmail. Admitting so wouldn't shed a positive light on either of them. The entire subject brought bitterness to her mouth. She sipped her margarita, sweetening up the sour subject. "We're mending fences, sort of."

"Are you two dating?"

"Well," Cara said, taking a deep breath, "I guess we are. We've gone on a few casual dates."

Alicia observed her carefully and Cara wanted to confide in her friend. She needed someone to talk to. Her mother was out of the question, and none of her friends in Dallas would understand her dating Kevin now when she'd been so adamant about getting on with her life. She added, "Actually, we're going out to dinner tomorrow night. And he's taking me to Lance's wedding reception."

"Sounds very hopeful," Alicia said.

The entrees were delivered to the table, releasing Cara from commenting further. They both dug into the salads. "So, what got you interested in working for the museum?" Cara asked. Alicia had mentioned she was the curator of the Somerset Museum of Natural History.

"I love history." Alicia shrugged with a little smile. "It's a small museum, but I enjoy getting up in the morning and going to work. There's so much history in this area."

Cara noted a gleam in Alicia's dark eyes when she spoke her work. "It's a fulfilling job."

Alicia nodded. "Yes, I feel fortunate."

Cara felt fortunate, too, at the moment. Alicia's sweet nature reminded her of all the good things in her life.

An image of Kevin popped into her head. They were getting closer each day. Was that one of the good things in her life?

Cara concentrated on shopping the rest of the afternoon. She and Alicia walked the long streets, entering various shops, an antique bookstore, a pottery store filled with hand-painted vases and plates, and an art gallery. As they strolled along sharing anecdotes, Cara remembered why she'd been so fond of Alicia. She was easy to be with and their conversation flowed naturally. Their last stop was Rebecca Huntington's lingerie boutique, Sweet Nothings.

"Wait until you see the gorgeous lingerie in here," Alicia said.

The minute Cara entered Somerset's newest shop she saw for herself what Alicia had meant. Lace, satin and silk lingerie in a variety of pastels was displayed throughout the shop. Cara took all of it in, noting the exquisite fabrics presented on satin hangers. Mirrored wall shelves showcased exotic perfumes. A sitting area with sofa and chairs surrounded a marble table set with delicate coffee cups and teapots for a little respite between shopping sprees. "How lovely," Cara said.

A woman with stunning red hair that was pulled

into a knot at the back of her head approached. With green eyes as warm as her manner, she greeted them. "Hello and welcome to Sweet Nothings." She looked at Alicia with a slight slant of her head. "You're Alejandro Montoya's sister, aren't you?"

"Yes, Alex is my brother. I'm Alicia. I've come into your shop a few times, but wasn't sure you recognized me. You're Rebecca Huntington, aren't you?"

Everyone at the Texas Cattleman's Club knew the Huntington name, of course. Her father, Sebastian Huntington, was one of the oldest members of the club and he was well-known but not well liked, from what Cara recalled.

Rebecca's eyes lost their glow for a second, then she nodded. "Yes. I was sorry to hear about your mother's death. Carmen was a lovely woman."

Emotion flitted through Alicia's gaze and Cara sensed a history between the two women, and not a good one.

"Is there anything I might show you?" Rebecca said, looking from Cara to Alicia. "Or would you like to browse?"

"Browsing, first," Cara said. "You have a lovely shop. I want to see *everything*."

Rebecca cast her a wide smile. "Thank you. Just let me know if you need any help."

Rebecca walked behind the counter to resume her duties, and Cara and Alicia ventured farther into the shop.

"Look at this," Alicia said, strolling to a rounder.

Her attitude warned that she didn't want to discuss her past relationship with Rebecca. She pulled out a hanger holding a skimpy, pink baby-doll two-piece set striped with black lace. She held it up for Cara to see.

"Oh, that would look great on you, with your olive skin."

Alicia let go a chuckle. "And where would I wear this? Or more exactly, for whom?"

"There's no one special in your life, Alicia?" Cara asked, keeping her voice low.

"No," she said. "There are days when I wonder if I'll ever have someone to wear such exquisite things for."

"How about for yourself? Pamper yourself a little."

Alicia glanced at the nightie one last time before quickly setting it back on its rounder. "Someday, maybe." But the longing in her voice belied her fast action. She turned her attention to Cara. "Maybe you should pick up something for your date with Kevin."

Cara smiled and glanced around the store, her gaze stopping on a rack that held one-of-a-kind black-lace nighties. Cara wanted to blow Kevin's mind with a naughty number that would create a lifelong memory for them both. "I intend to, and you're gonna help me find just the right one. Come look at these over here."

Alicia followed her to the rack. Cara held up a garment that appealed to her and ran her hand inside to demonstrate how the fine, delicate, lacy threads would expose more skin than they covered. "What do you think?"

"Makes a statement," Alicia said with twinkling eyes.

Cara grinned. It was perfect. "I think so, too."

Alicia let go a deep sigh. "You're glowing." She looked at Cara with a tilt of her head, her voice filled with yearning. "Must be nice to be so much in love."

Love?

Had Cara fallen back in love with Kevin?

Cara's heart surged. Warmth spread through her body and the realization struck that she *was* in love with Kevin Novak. All over again. Maybe she'd never stopped loving him. And the night she'd wear this lingerie would be her last night with Kevin before they finalized a divorce that had been four years in the making.

Only now, she wasn't certain she wanted it at all.

Seven

Kevin glanced at his watch for the twentieth time today. In just three hours, he'd be picking Cara up for their date. Anticipation coursed through his body, making him impatient and eager.

He peered down at the completed files on his desk. Working like a madman today, he'd managed to get through most everything in record time and hold a team meeting for his latest apartment complex project on the outskirts of Houston. He had a few notes to make about the project before turning them in to legal.

He was just finishing up his last thoughts when Darius and Lance walked in, unannounced. Kevin glanced past them to the opened door and his secretary, Marin, who sat at her desk. "Can't get decent help these days. She lets just anybody walk into my office."

"I heard that," Marin called out. "You're lucky to have me."

"Yeah, you're lucky to have her," Darius said with a wide grin.

"We came to deliver you from all this," Lance said, sweeping his right arm over Kevin's paper-laden desk. "It's happy hour, starting right now."

Kevin twisted his mouth, stood up and walked to the door. "Kidding," he said unnecessarily to his secretary. She'd been advised to never hold Lance or Darius in the outer office unless he was in a meeting. He closed the door and looked at his friends. "Can't. Not tonight."

"Why not?" Darius asked.

"I've got a date in a few hours."

"With Cara?"

Kevin folded his arms over his middle. "That's right."

Darius shook his head. "I know what you're up to. I recognize all the signs. You're trying to get back at Cara for hurting you. But trust me, it's only gonna come back to bite you in the ass."

"It's something I need to do," Kevin said in his own defense. "What makes you such an expert?"

"I did the same thing with Summer. I wanted revenge for what she did to me seven years ago, but I hurt myself in the process by denying my love for her. I almost lost her, Kevin."

"My situation's different."

"If you're that angry and hurt, it's only because you're still in love with her and won't admit it."

Lance agreed with Darius. "I think you should listen to him, Kev. You'll see it more clearly over a good drink."

"Yeah, well, maybe I'm changing my mind about having drinks with you two."

Lance scrubbed his chin.

Both men grabbed him by the elbow, one on each side, and bulldozed him out of his office. "Maybe if we'd have pulled you out of your office more, back in the day, you two would still be together. On your way to making us uncles," Darius added.

Kevin yanked his arms free and regained his composure just before reaching his secretary's desk. "We're closing up early. Go on home and have a good night," he said, ignoring Lance's and Darius's smug smiles.

"Thanks, Mr. Novak."

They rode the elevator down. "Five years ago, I'd have punched both of you out for trying that stunt."

Darius threw his head back and laughed heartily. "You would've tried, Novak. But not succeeded."

"Five years ago," Lance began, "you never would've stopped working, not even for a drink with friends."

"Meaning?"

Lance cocked his head and shrugged his broad shoulders. "Meaning, you're making progress. Though you're a slow learner."

Kevin shook his head. "You guys don't let up."

"C'mon," Lance said, stepping off the elevator. "The bar is calling. We won't make you late for your date with Cara."

"Better not." What Kevin wouldn't tell them was that his plan had already worked. Cara was falling for him again. He saw it in the soft way she looked at him now and in the sweet tone of her voice when they spoke on the phone. "The last thing I want to do is tick her off."

By eight-fifteen, Cara was pacing the floor of her hotel room. At eight-thirty, she glanced at the phone on the nightstand, then pulled out her cell phone and gave it a sour look. Kevin had been due to pick her up half an hour ago. He hadn't called. Cara vacillated about whether to call him or not. But rising anger won out. She slammed her phone shut and tossed it back into her purse.

"He knows how to reach me," she muttered.

Cara's mind rewound to all those days he'd come home later than she'd expected, all those dinners she'd worked on meticulously going untouched. The lonely nights she'd waited up for him. And later, the lonely nights when she'd gone to bed before he'd come home. She'd begun to think it was her. After all, all the other young married women she knew had husbands who came home like clockwork. They ate their dinners together. They spent their weekends doing fun things. She'd found herself longing for Kevin, when it was obvious he hadn't longed for her.

He'd never needed her company, not like that. Not like most newlyweds, who couldn't get enough of each other. She'd begun to feel inadequate as a wife, like she couldn't keep her husband interested. Her feelings had escalated when she'd wanted to have a baby and Kevin had kept putting it off. "There's time for that. We're young yet."

She'd been a sucker then, forgiving him after each excuse, until finally after years of hearing him out, his excuses had fallen on deaf ears. At least she was grateful they hadn't had children. She didn't want to raise a child in a broken home. Because when the pain had gotten too strong, Cara had had no option but to leave, and salvage what was left of her heart.

She wondered what excuse he'd come up with now. And then lightning struck.

"I'm not sticking around to find out."

Cara wasn't the understanding, innocent young wife she once had been. She grabbed her purse and took a quick look at herself in the mirror. Dressed in her little black dress, her blond curls resting on her shoulders, she gave herself an approving nod before walking out the door.

With each step she took, her anger rose. She rode the elevator down to the lobby and headed straight for the concierge desk. She found a middle-aged man with a kind face standing behind the counter.

"I'd like a cab. Where can I find a nice place to listen to music and have a drink?"

The concierge, whose name tag revealed his name was George, smiled. "Well, a cab might not be necessary. The Fairfield Room is available to our guests tonight and the band is scheduled to go on in a few minutes."

"Perfect," Cara said. She could have a drink or two and not worry about finding her way back to the hotel. "Just point me in the right direction."

"I'll do better than that," he said, coming around the counter. "I'll walk you there myself."

Kevin knocked on Cara's door at precisely eight forty-five. He was late picking her up, but it couldn't be helped. After having one drink with Lance and Darius, he'd gotten a call from the night watchman at the apartment complex project. The apartment structure had been vandalized. Teddy Burford had been roughed up a bit and knocked unconscious for a few seconds.

Kevin had given the elderly night-guard the job personally. He was a war veteran who'd been qualified for the job and he had sensed the old guy needed to feel useful in his later years. Kevin stayed with Teddy while he gave the police his story. Nothing was stolen and, from Teddy's description of the culprits, it appeared to have been a teenage prank. Teddy had startled three boys. They'd panicked and one of the boys had shoved him hard. He'd hit his head against the wall and blacked out for a few moments.

Kevin had waited with Teddy until his daughter had picked him up to take him to the emergency room for observation. Then he'd finally glanced at his watch. When he'd realized he'd be late for his date with Cara, he'd called her immediately. She hadn't answered her phone.

Now he stood outside her door, knocking more loudly the second time. "Cara, it's Kevin."

No answer.

He let go a vivid curse and knocked one more time before leaving. He dialed her cell phone number again on his way to the elevator and it went straight to voice mail. She'd turned off her phone.

In the lobby, Kevin spoke with two bellmen, then three women behind the registration desk. One of the employees pointed out the concierge.

Kevin nodded and headed his way. "Excuse me, but I'm looking for my wife, Mrs. Novak. Blond, about so high—" he gestured to her five-foot-eight height "—and beautiful."

George looked him over carefully, then nodded. "I just walked your wife over to the Fairfield Room. It's on the third floor just off the—"

"Thanks." Kevin took off before the concierge finished giving him directions. He'd planned on being with Cara tonight and nothing was going to stop him. Even though he might have to grovel a bit, he'd make her understand why he'd been late.

Kevin followed the sounds of live music, a soft, sultry ballad leading him easily enough to the Fairfield Room. He stood in the double-door entrance to a room with elegant swag draperies, Venetian chandeliers that sparkled like diamonds and a dark wood, parquet dance floor. People huddled around the long bar. Kevin leaned casually against the doorjamb, arms folded, in search of his wife.

When he spotted her, he lifted away slightly to get a better look at Cara in the arms of a stranger, slow-dancing and making conversation.

She looked beautiful in her little black dress and long, glittering earrings, showing enough leg to make a grown man cry.

Kevin tried to temper his frustration, yet the voice in his head wouldn't let it go.

What did you expect?

She's young and beautiful and once you sign those papers, she'll be free to date other men.

Get used to it, buddy.

When the man dancing with Cara brought her up closer, Kevin's frustration transformed into something that made him stride into the room with deliberate steps. His gaze pinned solely on Cara, he walked up to her and set a hand on her arm. She whirled around, her eyes wide.

"Sorry I'm late, babe."

Her mouth dropped open. "Kevin."

She glanced at the man she'd been dancing with and smiled apologetically.

He gave her a quizzical look, then spoke to Kevin. "We're in the middle of a dance."

"I'm aware of that." Kevin couldn't fault the guy for his attempt at chivalry. "But you're dancing with my wife." He cocked the man a smile. "I can take over now."

The man stared at Kevin, then darted a glance at Cara's ringless left finger before dropping his arms from her.

"Soon to be divorced," she added in explanation. The man nodded and lingered. A tic worked at Kevin's jaw.

"Nice meeting you, Cara."

"Same here, Dylan. Sorry about the interruption."

Kevin's patience ebbed. "If you'll excuse us, I need to speak with my wife."

"Sure thing." Dylan eyed Cara once more before walking off the dance floor.

"That wasn't pretty, Kevin." Cara's eyes darkened.

"Maybe not, but it's justified. I'm apologizing for being late."

"Apology declined." Cara marched off the dance floor.

Kevin rolled his eyes and had a good mind not to follow her, but damn it, she'd hear his explanation and then she could decide to be angry or not.

She walked to a table and picked up her purse, tucking it under her arm. "You ruined my evening, Kevin. And you ruined a perfectly nice dance I was enjoying."

"With *that* guy?" Kevin pointed in the direction of the dance floor.

Cara ignored his question. "As I recall, it was you who wanted me to be in town for these weeks, pending our divorce. The least you could do is *show up* when you say you will."

Kevin took a deep breath. "Let's sit down and I'll explain."

"Kevin, don't you see? I don't want your explanations. I heard all of your excuses years ago."

"Okay, if you won't sit down, then dance with me."

"Kevin," she said, exasperated. She ran a hand through her hair and looked away.

He stroked her cheek and she turned to face him. He smiled and said softly, "I'm sorry. I called you as soon as I could."

"I was always second best."

He heard the pain in her voice.

It was important to him that she understood what had happened tonight. She'd always accused him of not putting her first, when that's exactly what he'd done. She'd left him for ill-conceived reasons and he wouldn't let her go to bed tonight thinking she'd been right all those years ago and right tonight as well.

The band played a mellow tune. He took her purse from her and set it down on the chair. "One dance. I'll tell you what happened tonight. I'll tell you about Teddy Burford. Then you can decide what happens next."

Cara's pretty blue eyes gave away her curiosity. "Who's Teddy Burford?"

"Dance with me, and I'll tell you."

"Blackmailing me again?" She whispered the question with a slight tilt of her head and the sweetest curve of her lips.

Kevin's resolve bumped up a notch. He stared at her soft pink lips. "Seems to be the only way with you."

"Not true," she said as she started toward the dance floor. "But I do enjoy dancing."

He watched the sexy twitch of her hips as she moved without him on the dance floor. Without another second of hesitation, he took her into his arms, bringing her up close, her body flush with his. "Ah, Cara. You feel good." He ran his hands up and down her sides, from shoulder to hip.

"Uh-huh." She took his hands and planted them firmly on her hips. She wrapped her arms around his neck and leaned back. "So what happened tonight?"

Kevin explained how he'd first met Teddy Burford when they'd been renovating the Community Senior Center. Teddy had sat among bingo-playing women, looking miserable. He'd lost his wife the year before and was living with his daughter. Though she hadn't complained, Teddy had felt as though he was intruding on her family life.

"I'd meet him for lunch and he'd tell me his war stories. He served two tours of duty in 'Nam. Earned a few medals, too. I kept thinking it was a shame that he wasted his days at the senior center. He'd told me he'd been looking for work, but he wasn't having any luck. You know, he wanted some financial independence. Anyone would want that."

"But he was too old?"

"Only in years. Not in heart. So when the night watchman job came up at the apartment complex, I told him to apply. I didn't want him to think I was giving him the job, but I knew I would. He's a tough old guy with military experience. He knows his stuff."

"Sounds to me, you might have given him the job, regardless," she mused.

"Lucky for me, he was qualified. And he appreciated the work."

"I like him already," Cara said.

"I was having a drink with Lance and Darius tonight when he called. He sounded pretty shaken up."

Kevin went on to explain about the vandals and Teddy's injuries. "Really, Cara, the old guy is my friend. I didn't go there for any other reason but to make sure he was okay. He was distraught, not about having been knocked out, but because he didn't protect the property. He thought he'd failed me and I assured him he did his job and then some. I stayed with him until his daughter picked him up. By that time, I was late calling you. I know I should have called you sooner, but—"

Cara shook her head. "I get it, Kevin. You did the right thing. But even you have to understand why I'd think the worst. You've left me standing alone a hundred times in the past, so why should I have thought any differently tonight?"

Kevin inhaled the fresh citrus scent of her hair and closed his eyes. "You were never second-best, Cara."

Kevin felt the exact moment Cara surrendered. Her shoulders loosened, her body relaxed and she put her head on his shoulder. "Just dance with me, Kevin."

He tightened his hold on her, satisfied that she'd understood and forgiven him. They didn't have much time left together and he wanted to make the most of every minute.

Two hours later, the band called it quits. Cara stood on the dance floor facing Kevin, her body sizzling. They'd had drinks and danced through the night. Cara had a sneaking feeling that Kevin had paid off the band to play only slow, sultry tunes. The music, sweet to her ears, and swaying to each song in Kevin's strong arms was a heady mix she couldn't deny.

Kevin's lips constantly brushed her forehead, his warm breath caressed her throat and his hands roamed to places on her body that were just this side of decent. She moved against him and taught him to seduce the music. And in turn, he'd very nearly seduced her.

She ached for him. Deep down. Not only had she forgiven him but his friendship with a down-and-out, lonely war veteran endeared him to her even more.

"It's getting late." Everyone on the dance floor had dispersed. The band began packing up their gear.

Kevin nodded. "The night didn't turn out as I'd planned. It was even better. Did you have a good time?"

Cara closed her eyes briefly and sighed. "Yes. I love dancing." She loved being with him. They'd talked and laughed, and then got hot and bothered in each other's arms. "Thank you."

"We'd better leave before they kick us out," he said.

A uniformed clean-up crew had entered and were removing the tablecloths from the tables.

"Did you know Pavoratti once sang in this very room?"

Kevin shook his head as they walked to their table. He handed over her purse. "Didn't know that."

"George told me on the way up here."

"Ah, George, the concierge. I think he was smitten with you."

"No, just a nice man."

"Cara, there are no *nice* men. Not when it comes to a beautiful woman. I thought I'd have to fight off that Dylan character just to get a dance with you."

They walked toward the elevator. "You used the wife card, instead."

Kevin let go a chuckle. "Worked like a charm."

"Technically, I'm not your wife. Or I won't be in a few days."

Kevin's tone changed instantly. "Would you rather I'd socked the guy in the jaw?"

Cara laughed. "You wouldn't."

One brow lifted and his eyes narrowed. "I would."

Cara walked on. Kevin wrapped his hand around

hers as they headed to the elevator. "I can make it to my room from here."

"I'll walk you." His jaw firm, his tone determined, she wouldn't argue.

They stepped into the elevator and the second the doors closed Kevin backed her up against the wall. "I've been waiting all night to do this."

One hand flattened against the elevator wall while the other hand wound around to the back of her head, bringing her face close to his. His mouth swooped down and he crushed his lips to hers.

Pent-up tension uncurled in the pit of her stomach. She welcomed the release, craving him with fiery need. His lips sought hers again and again and she matched each kiss with equal ferocity. The sharp taste of hard alcohol mingled with his breath. Her heart pounded and goose bumps rose up her arms.

He dropped his head, bringing his lips to her throat, nibbling, nipping. She curled her fingers in his short, thick hair and allowed him access. He kissed the swells of her breasts, then brought his hands around to caress each one through the material of her dress. His touch made her toes curl. Her nipples stood at full attention. He slid his fingers over the tips, and heat surged through her body.

"Kevin," she cooed, his name slipping from her lips.

The elevator continued to climb and he continued his assault, his kisses frenzied now. Cara huffed out quick breaths, wrapped up in the thrilling moment.

Kevin hiked up the hem of her dress and stroked her along her inner thigh. Rapid-fire sensations shot up her leg, making every cell in her body alert and aware. She moaned from the sheer pleasure, Kevin's hands roaming all over her, his kisses hot and wet and determined.

His erection pulsed against her.

Oh, no, she thought. We can't make love in the elevator. Can we?

The elevator dinged. She froze and looked at the digital display above the doors. She'd reached her floor.

Kevin backed away from her and composed himself.

The doors opened. Luckily, no one was on the other side. Both of them looked disheveled, hair mussed, clothes awry as if…as if they'd had sex in the elevator.

Cara quickly stepped out and looked at Kevin.

His back against the elevator wall, he cast her a crooked smile.

He looked adorable, like a mischievous schoolboy who'd gotten away with ditching class.

"Just four more days, baby."

Heat crawled up her neck. Cara nodded, unable to say a word, but picturing the night they'd finally make love. Kevin hit a button and the doors closed, leaving Cara alone on the hotel floor, hot, bothered and angry with herself for having made this deal with Kevin in the first place.

Four more days before they'd satisfy their desire.

And four more days before Cara was a free woman.

She didn't know which of the two worried her the most.

Eight

"All right, Marissa. I'll see you in a few days." Cara hung up the phone after averting a disaster with two of her most talented dance instructors. Both had threatened to quit and Cara spent the entire morning consoling each one, listening to their complaints about the other and asking them to hold on until she could talk with them in person.

Felicia and Marissa were as temperamental as they come. When Cara was in Dallas, she managed to keep the peace between them. Quite frankly, she was tired of being their intermediary and babysitter. When she returned, she'd lay down the law. If they wanted to continue working at Dancing Lights, they'd have to get along. Period. Cara would hate to lose either one of them, but she'd learned that professionalism was not only admirable but necessary in her employees. She'd learned a good deal about owning a business in the past few years. But she'd always vowed never to allow her business to dominate her personal life.

Her thoughts turned to Kevin. *He* was her personal life right now. For the next four days, anyway. She'd had a great time with him last night. Even though the evening had begun badly, he had managed to turn the night around to become something she would long remember. If there had been any doubt before, being with him last night had convinced her that she'd fallen for him again.

"I love you, Kevin," she whispered in the quiet of her hotel room. She could hardly believe her own revelation. Cara closed her eyes, refusing tears.

Grateful that he was out of town today, Cara could spend the rest of the day trying to sort out her feelings. She'd go online to get some work done, shop for a wedding gift for Lance and Kate, and spend the evening alone with her thoughts.

She needed the time to think things through. She'd get the divorce she'd come to Houston for, but was that what she really wanted? Was she guilty of the same thing she'd accused Kevin of doing, putting business before her personal life? Should she try to work things out with her husband? He hadn't given her any indication of what he wanted for the future. Cara had one day to mull over her situation before

Kevin would knock on her door to take her to Lance and Kate's wedding reception. One day to figure out what she wanted for the rest of her life.

At precisely six-thirty the next evening, Kevin stood at Cara's door wearing a three-piece tuxedo in James Bond fashion. No, she amended—he looked better than 007, and Cara had to purse her lips tight to keep her mouth from dropping open. In black from head to toe, except for the silver-gray tie tucked into his vest, Cara had never seen a more handsome man.

He's my husband.

And I'm standing here drooling.

"I missed you yesterday," were the first words he spoke.

Cara had a hard time keeping her ego from floating off into space.

"I had a contractual meeting in Austin that had been planned months ago or I would have cancelled in a heartbeat."

"I understand." He really had no obligation to see her every day, yet he'd called her three times yesterday when he'd had free time.

"You look beautiful. Red is my favorite color on you." His gaze stayed on her glossy-red lips for a long moment, then drifted down to her off-the-shoulder dress, then farther down to her red heels. "I bet your toenails are red, too."

Cara kicked off one shoe and wiggled her toes. "You guessed right. Candy-cane red."

"Ah, Cara." He grabbed her hips and brought her close, then bent his head to lay a mind-boggling kiss on her lips. Staying close, his mouth just a breath away, he whispered, "Don't invite me in."

Cara blinked.

"Lance would never forgive me if I showed up late. But he's gonna owe me one, big-time."

Cara chuckled and took his arm. "Then maybe we'd better go."

"Yeah, I was afraid you'd say that."

Twenty minutes later, they pulled up to the Texas Cattleman's Club. A valet opened the door to the Jag and helped Cara out. Kevin handed the valet his keys and was beside her instantly, putting a solid hand on her lower back. He guided her inside and they entered the formal dining room.

Two tall, white columns draped with deep-red rose arrangements stood in invitation at each side of the entrance. White tablecloths and flowered centerpieces in rich earth tones of red, amber and wine decorated each table. Twinkling lights illuminated the arched cathedral window and a dozen round pillar candles lit the carved travertine-stone fireplace mantel. Soft music from a four-piece orchestra played in the background. "Wow, it's stunning."

Kevin glanced around the room, then turned to her. "You make it so."

Her heart did a little flip. "Thank you," she whispered. Kevin had been so complimentary lately and so attentive that she could barely relate him to the man she'd left four years ago, or the man who'd blackmailed her into this two-week charade.

He escorted her farther into the room and she set her gift on a table. "What did you get them?" he asked.

"Personalized wineglasses and a wine tour."

"A wine tour?"

"A bottle of wine delivered each month of their first year of marriage from different regions of France and Italy."

Kevin nodded. "Very original. I'm sure they'll love it."

"Hmm, I hope so. It's hard choosing a gift when you've been out of the loop as long as I have." With a tilt of her head, she looked into Kevin's eyes. "I bet you chose a perfect gift for them."

Kevin shrugged. "I made a sizable donation in their name to their favorite charity."

Cara rocked back on her heels, overwhelmed at Kevin's sensitivity. "That's…very generous."

"I think they'll appreciate it."

A butler served them a glass of merlot and Kevin made a private toast. "To you, Cara. I hope all your dreams come true."

"And to you, Kevin," she said, offering a sentiment of her own. "I hope you find happiness."

They touched glasses gently and looked into each other's eyes as they took a sip.

Kevin remarked, "I'm pretty happy now."

So was she.

Cara's stomach clenched. Blood drained from her

face. Could she give all of this up? Could she divorce Kevin and not wonder if she'd made the worst mistake of her life? Was being with Kevin her real dream? He'd courted her for days now yet he hadn't said one word to lead her to think he wanted to reconcile.

"Anything wrong?" he asked.

"What could be wrong?" Cara answered quickly, pasting a smile on her face.

A tic worked in Kevin's jaw. That same tic that had always come out when they'd argued. He lowered his voice and his tone grew serious. "Yeah, what could be wrong?"

Justin Dupree walked up with a young, leggy blond woman. Cara recognized her immediately as Mila Jankovich, a supermodel she'd seen on a dozen magazines lately. Justin had classic good looks, a handsome profile and dynamic blue eyes, and the two together made an eye-catching couple. Introductions were made and more wine was poured as they conversed.

Mila seemed infatuated with Justin, being years his junior, Cara presumed. And though she'd always thought Justin a nice guy, he had a reputation with women. No father in his right mind would like to see Justin Dupree courting his daughter.

The orchestra quieted and an announcement was made when Kate and Lance entered the room. The small crowd of friends and family applauded.

Kate beamed with joy and Lance had never looked happier. Cara's heart sank even further. She remembered her own wedding and the brightness that had filled her when she and Kevin had spoken their vows. She'd had hopes of a happy future, with a new husband and children someday. None of that had happened for her. Yet, here she was, standing beside Kevin, unsure of their relationship.

Should she tell him she loved him?

Or should she take him at his word, that he wanted to part as friends?

Friends?

She didn't want him as a friend. Not anymore. She wanted more. She'd seen the changes in Kevin and believed that he was a different man than the one who'd hurt her so terribly.

Could she trust in that?

Kevin held Cara in his arms on the dance floor, the orchestra strings creating a romantic mood. He breathed in her exotic scent and threaded his fingers into her blond curls. He had trouble holding on to his bitter need for revenge when he had her in his arms. Soft and feminine and the most beautiful woman in the room, Cara made him forget all the pain she'd caused him. Kevin had never had a woman run out on him before. He'd never been left holding the bag, racked by humiliation, his pride shredded to pieces. He remembered those drunken days after she'd first left, the ache of desolation mixing with anger and frustration. He remembered having to tell his parents and friends the truth. He'd hated their pity and sympathy. He'd felt like a failure in his personal life, when he'd been nothing but successful in his professional life.

Those feelings had stayed with him for four years. His resentment was fueled even more by the reason she'd come back for a divorce—to get a bank loan. He'd seduced her for the past eleven days with one goal in mind, and he wasn't a man to deviate from a plan once it was constructed. But perhaps he'd laid out his plan too well because he was softening to her.

"Are you okay?" she asked, her blond brows furrowing.

"I'm fine." He gave her a reassuring smile.

Darius tapped him on the shoulder. "Mind if I cut in?"

Yeah, he minded, but Cara had already released him. "Darius, I'd love to dance with you."

Kevin relented, turning Cara over to Darius. He took up his glass of wine and found it lacking in alcohol content. He headed to the bar in search of a stronger drink, needing a moment to get a grip, to back off from feelings he wanted no part of. Lance came up beside him and leaned one arm against the bar, facing him.

"Whiskey, straight up," Kevin told the bartender. "And bring the groom one, too."

Lance laughed. "Cara's getting to you, isn't she?"

"Nice party, Lance." Kevin refused to take the bait.

"Glad you're enjoying yourself. Cara seems to be, too."

"She's having a nice enough time."

"You haven't let her out of your sight for two hours."

Kevin scratched the back of his neck. "Are you keeping track?"

The bartender slid two drinks their way. Lance smirked before he took a sip of his drink. "Hell, I saw the look you shot Darius when he interrupted your dance. If looks could kill…"

"She's only here a few more days."

"Are you still working on your brilliant plan to get back at her?"

Kevin winced. He lifted his glass to his lips. "Maybe."

"Man, don't be stupid."

"Shut up, Lance."

"Am I hitting too close to home? Are you having doubts? If you are, then I'd say you're making progress."

"You have no idea what you're talking about."

"I know you were hurt, Kev. I know you thought she abandoned you. But did you ever consider her side? Maybe both of you were right and both of you were wrong."

Kevin sucked in oxygen. "I'm so glad I came to your wedding reception. Does Kate know what a nosy-body she married?"

"She knows I love my friends."

"Two more whiskeys," Kevin said to the bartender, then turned to Lance. "Do me a favor, don't love me so much."

"Funny, Kev. You're a real comedian."

Kevin nodded. "Whether you think so or not, I know what I'm doing."

Lance sipped his second whiskey and put a hand on Kevin's shoulder. "That, my friend, remains to be seen."

When Kevin returned to the table, Darius and Summer approached, along with Justin, Mila and Mitch Brody. They all sat down, and Summer and Cara struck up a conversation.

"What gave you the idea to develop a chain of dance studios?" Summer asked Cara.

Cara's eyes sparkled. "Well, I'd always loved to dance. I studied several forms of dance as a young girl. Ballet, of course, but swing, too, and some ballroom and I…well, I—" She glanced at Kevin, then shrugged and sipped her drink.

"With all the dance competitions on television now, I imagine it's very sought after in the real world," Summer said.

Cara nodded, her smile wide. "There's a good-size market out there now. People want to feel good about themselves. There's nothing more freeing to me than moving with the music."

"You do it well," Darius added. He looked to Summer. "She gave me some pointers when we danced."

Cara chuckled. "Oh, no. I'm not taking credit for that. Darius has enough rhythm for a three-piece jazz band. He could very well be on my staff as an instructor."

"Right," Darius said with a shake of his head. "I'd probably scare off your clients."

Summer laid a hand on his arm. "Darius is a man of many talents."

"You keep saying that," Justin chimed in with a twinkle in his blue eyes, "but no one else sees it."

Darius feigned an angry look. "Careful, pretty boy."

Kevin listened as his friends bantered back and forth, for the most part keeping quiet. Cara shot him curious looks from time to time while she engaged in conversation. He noted the strong, confident woman she'd become. She'd always been intelligent and clever, but Cara had grown in other ways and, more and more, he liked what he saw in her. And as she spoke with Summer about her social work and the Texas Cattleman's Club shelter, Helping Hands, the two discussed how to best serve the community. It was clear Cara had made a new friend.

But Cara wouldn't have time to develop that friendship. It would all end soon. After they consummated their deal, he'd sign the divorce papers and let her go, his revenge complete.

And by letting her go, he'd be free, too.

To move on with his life.

Yet Lance's words kept reverberating in his head. *Don't be stupid, Kevin.*

Am I hitting too close to home?

Are you having doubts?

Damn it, yes. He had doubts. He had feelings for

Cara that he couldn't deny. The more he tried to push them out of his mind, the stronger they'd become.

Thankfully, Mitch Brody interrupted his train of thought. "How about a game of tennis tomorrow after work?"

"Yeah, sure." He'd make the time. Maybe knocking a ball around would knock some sense into his head.

Twenty minutes later, Cara slipped away from the party to use the ladies' room. She needed a breather from Kevin and the thoughts of reconciliation that kept entering her head. Being on his arm tonight, meeting up with old friends, more and more she felt like she could slide right into the role as wife to Kevin. He'd changed from the type-A personality businessman he'd been, driven to succeed no matter the cost to his personal life. He'd made his millions and, with nothing more to prove, he seemed to have figured out how to keep an equal balance between business and pleasure.

It felt right being here with him and feeling a part of the Somerset community again. A swirl of excitement coursed through her system. Caught up in the festivities and the romance of Kate and Lance's wedding reception, Cara felt like she belonged.

She entered the ladies' room lobby. "Cara!"

Cara faced Alicia Montoya in the large, gilded vanity mirror. Alicia swirled around with lipstick in midair to face her directly.

"Alicia, hi! It's good to see you."

Alicia set her tube of lipstick down and they embraced. "What a nice surprise."

"I'm here with Kevin. Remember I told you about Lance and Kate's wedding reception?"

"Yes, I know. Alex and I were having dinner in the café and we could hear you all having a great time."

"We are." Then Cara lowered her voice. "Especially me. It's been a really wonderful night."

Alicia leaned in. "Wonderful enough to use your new Sweet Nothing purchase?"

Cara chuckled. "Who knows what the night might bring?" She wouldn't explain that she'd wear her new lingerie the night she and Kevin made love, in a few days. Not before. She really wanted to knock his socks off and make a lasting memory.

Alicia bubbled with excitement. "I may have to make a trip back to that store soon. I just met the most dreamy man here at TCC and he asked me out."

"Oh, Alicia. That's great. Who is he?"

Alicia's face took on a glow and her dark brows lifted. "His name is Rick Jones. We had a brief conversation outside while I was waiting for Alex. I would have remembered if I'd seen him before. He's not a man a woman could forget. Not with those amazing blue eyes."

"Well, you'll have to spill all the details after your date. I'm dying to hear how it all works out."

"No more than me, Cara. I haven't had a date in a while. And, well, Rick is charming and handsome. He's attending the wedding reception."

"Oh, really?" Cara tried to figure out which of the partygoers could be Rick Jones, but she came up short. Though the reception was relatively small, Cara didn't know all of Kate and Lance's friends.

"I've been floating all night, driving Alex crazy with my good mood."

Cara took her hand and couldn't stop the grin that pulled at her mouth. "Good for you. For being happy, that is, not for driving Alex crazy."

Cara couldn't blame a man for being attracted to Alicia's sweet demeanor and beautiful looks. Cara had always admired her light olive skin tone and dazzling brown eyes. Tonight, she looked stunning in a simple, brown, off-the-shoulder sweater and pencil skirt, her dark hair swept back in curls. "Whoever this Rick Jones is, he's a lucky guy."

Alicia hugged her again. "Thanks, Cara. I'd better go before Alex thinks I deserted him."

"Okay. Enjoy the rest of your evening. We'll talk soon."

"Yes, we will. Have a good time tonight with Kevin." Alicia wiggled her fingers in a farewell wave and dashed out of the ladies' room.

Cara returned to the reception minutes later, surprised to find the orchestra had ceased playing, replaced by piped-in rock music. Alcohol flowed in abundance, the dance floor was in full swing and the small crowd filled the room with laughter and shouts to the bride and groom. She found Kevin swinging the young supermodel around on the dance floor, the lanky blonde laughing heartily and sipping her drink.

Cara's heart sank seeing Kevin with another woman, seeming to enjoy the attention she bestowed him. Cara searched the reception for Justin Dupree but couldn't find him anywhere.

When the music ended, Kevin headed her way. "Hey, I thought you'd never come back."

Cara granted him a quick smile, concealing the jealousy she felt seeing Kevin with Mila. He was by Cara's side again now, giving her his full attention. "I ran into a friend in the ladies' room. What happened to the orchestra?"

Kevin grinned. "Lance made a deal with Kate. A few hours of sedate orchestra music, then we let our hair down."

"Wow. Now it looks like a party."

"Yeah, an open bar and heavy rock can do that to a perfectly good wedding reception." Kevin glanced at Mitch Brody. "I think they're ready for the toasts. C'mon," he said, taking her arm. "I want you next to me when I roast Lance."

"Over a fire pit?"

A wicked smirk crossed his features and Kevin's eyes gleamed. "Yeah, something like that."

But after Mitch's toast to his brother, amid whistles and hoots from the boisterous crowd, a stern-looking man entered the room and spoke directly to Lance.

Cara watched Lance argue with the man, shaking

his head until Kate put her hand on Lance's arm. Lance spoke briefly with Kate and then rose to speak with their guests. "Apparently, we're having too much fun in here for someone at the club. Complaints have been lodged from the room next door about the noise level and we've been asked to leave."

The entire room groaned in unison.

"I know, I know," Lance said, holding his apparent anger in check.

Kate rose and spoke to her guests. "This has been an amazing party, and Lance and I want to thank all of you for coming. I can't tell you how much it means to both of us to have our dearest friends here to celebrate our marriage."

"Yes," Lance said. "Thank you all for coming, but Kate and I don't want the party to end. We're inviting all of you back to our place. And I promise you, we can make all the noise we want there!"

The crowd in the room applauded.

Cara turned to Kevin. "Can they do that? Break up the party because of noise?"

Kevin shrugged. "TCC has rigid rules and apparently whoever complained made a big stink about it. Lance is furious, but he's keeping his cool for Kate's sake. So, what do you say? Want to go to the after party with me?"

"I wouldn't miss it," Cara said, grinning.

The party guests followed Kate and Lance out the front entrance of the club. Kevin noticed Sebastian Huntington speaking with Cornelius Gentry under a streetlamp. Gentry, a wiry little man known to be Huntington's foreman, glanced over to the group. Both men wore smug expressions on their faces.

Immediately, Kevin's suspicions were aroused. Huntington, a snob in the worst way, hated the "new money" millionaires at the club. He didn't think they were good enough to rub noses with the elite of Houston and he never failed to make his feelings well known.

Kevin tightened his hold on Cara, squeezing her hand gently as they walked with the group toward the valet station to wait for his car.

Cara glanced up at him and smiled sweetly. Her smile made him forget his suspicions and he concentrated on how beautiful she looked tonight. He bent his head and kissed her lightly on the lips.

"What was that for?" she whispered.

A swell of possessiveness filled his heart. He looked into her soft blue eyes and couldn't come up with a witty reply. He opened his mouth to say something, but emotions overwhelmed him and sensations swept through his system as he realized his time with Cara was coming to an end.

"You son of a bitch!"

Kevin whirled around to find Lance marching toward Alex Montoya just outside the doors of the TCC. With each determined step he took, his eyes filled with more rage.

"You did this! You broke up my wedding reception!"

Alicia stood beside her brother, her eyes wide, her expression terrified.

Montoya stiffened and stared at Lance with hard eyes and tight lips. "What the hell are you talking about, Brody?" Alex took note of the guests standing behind Lance. Immediately, he shielded his sister by taking a step in front of her. Patience and understanding were not virtues in either man when they faced each other. It was bad enough that Lance believed Montoya had set fire to his refinery, but now Lance was accusing him of shutting down his wedding reception.

"You complained about the noise at my reception and had us all booted out of there!"

Alex's face flamed with indignation. "Now, why would I do that? I don't give a damn about your pathetic little wedding reception."

They stood nose-to-nose now, each man refusing to back off.

Kate watched the scene unfold, fear entering her eyes. "Oh, no."

"This is low, even for you." Lance glared at Alex.

"Watch it, Brody." Alex kept tight control of his temper. "Don't go making accusations you can't prove."

Alex turned around to take Alicia's arm. "Let's get out of here."

"Not so fast, Montoya. I'm not through with you!"

Slowly, Alex turned back around, his expression grim. He released his sister's arm. "You're not *through* with me?"

The situation had gone from bad to worse. Cara bit her lip and Kate appeared panicked. Lance and Alex were heading for trouble.

Kevin strode purposefully toward the two men. He faced them like a referee breaking up two linebackers ready to brawl. "Come on, Lance. Kate's upset. Let's not add to it."

Lance darted a glance at him. "Stay out of it, Kevin."

"Yeah, stay out of it, Novak." Montoya eyed him with disdain. "If the groom's got a bone to pick, I'm ready."

Lance gritted his teeth. "Damn right, I have a bone to pick."

Kevin scratched his head, wondering if he should let them have it out once and for all. They'd been rivals since high school and this would be the culmination of years of hatred and resentment. But one glance at Cara with those hope-filled blue eyes and Kevin knew what he had to do.

He stepped between them, facing Lance. "C'mon, man. Let's get out of here. Kate's waiting for you."

Lance inhaled sharply and peered around Kevin to cast Montoya a hard look. He took a long second to stare. Kevin held his breath. Finally, Lance relented. "This isn't over."

"Don't ever toss accusations at me again, Brody," Montoya warned with stern indignation. "But for the record, I had nothing to do with breaking up your party."

With that, he grabbed Alicia's arm and guided her back into the club.

"Bastard," Lance muttered.

Kate ran over to him. "Lance, are you crazy?"

Lance took one look at Kate's concerned face and threw his head back and laughed, finding humor in the situation. He reached for her, wrapped his arms around her waist and pulled her close. "Yeah, I'm crazy. About you. You deserve a beautiful wedding reception."

"And I got one. Tonight was wonderful. I enjoyed every single minute of it. Now, let's be good hosts. Our friends are waiting."

Lance glanced at the group who had witnessed his outburst. "The party's still on. At our house."

Satisfied, Kate kissed him lightly, then turned to Kevin. She mouthed a silent thank-you to him and he nodded.

Cara strode over and slipped her hand under his arm. "My hero."

Kevin glanced into her pretty eyes.

"You averted a disaster," she said.

"Heroes do that." He grinned, making light of the situation, yet couldn't shake his gut feeling that there was more to all this than met the eye.

Nine

The after party continued into the wee hours of the night. Cara and Kevin found a cozy corner of the living room and stayed cuddled together, kissing like two high-school teenagers who couldn't get enough of each other. When the party wound down, just the four of them remained. "I think we should give the newlyweds some privacy now."

Kevin glanced around, just noticing that they were the last of the guests. "Yeah, I bet they want to get to bed." He shot Cara a sizzling look, lowering his voice and leaning in. "I want to get you to bed, too."

His hot kiss erupted tingles on her arms. It had been like that all night—steamy kisses and smoldering glances and enough innuendo to bring her fantasies to life.

Fantasies of loving Kevin wholly and completely.

It had been nearly two weeks of torture. Two weeks of wondering, of being tempted beyond belief and two weeks of needing to quench the thirst she had for her husband.

Lance walked up with a crystal whiskey decanter in hand. "Ready for another?" he asked Kevin.

Kevin rose and took Cara's hand. "No, thanks. I think we're going to let you two get to bed."

Lance laughed, swaying a little. He grabbed Kate and kissed her smack on the lips. "Good idea."

"I think he's partied a little too hard tonight," Kate said, patting his arm lovingly.

Lance swayed a bit more and Kate wrapped her arms around his waist to steady him.

"Just…happy," Lance said, slurring his words slightly and casting Kate a crooked, silly smile.

"I can get him to the bedroom for you, Kate. It'll be like old times back at UT," Kevin offered.

"Nah," Lance said. "Don't need your services tonight, Kev. My wife knows how to take care of me." He wiggled his brows in villainous style.

Kate chuckled. "Well, I'm learning."

"You're a lucky man." Kevin slapped Lance on the back. Lance disengaged from Kate and smiled at him. "Kate, will you walk Kevin to the door?" Lance turned to Cara and offered his arm. "Cara?"

She slipped her arm through his and he tottered a

bit before straightening up. He waited until Kate and Kevin were steps ahead of them, then looked at Cara through lowered lashes. "Kevin's a good guy," he leaned in to whisper, his words running together. "Damn hardheaded though…I warned him to be careful…not to hurt you."

"How will he hurt me?" Cara asked, confused and wondering if she should pay attention to anything he said while intoxicated.

"I think he already has." Lance mumbled a curse, then shook his head as if shaking off cobwebs. "Never mind. Forget I said anything." He placed her hand in his and smiled warmly, then walked her to the front door.

That night, the last thing Cara could do was forget Lance's comments. She replayed his parting words over and over in her head, trying to make sense of them. He may have had too much to drink, but Lance wasn't so intoxicated that he didn't know what he was saying. She heard his true concern in the sobering way he whispered in her ear. What bothered her the most wasn't that she stood to get hurt by Kevin, but that Lance had knowledge of it. What was going on? What had Kevin said to Lance to make him believe she'd get hurt?

Or had Lance simply been way off in his assessment of the situation? Cara tossed on those thoughts before falling asleep that night.

In the morning, with sunshine pouring into her window and all things looking bright, she rose early, worked out to a Pilates exercise program on the flat screen and felt too happy to worry about anything. She'd spend the afternoon with Kevin today. They'd made those arrangements during the reception and, after a spellbinding good-night kiss, he'd reminded her that they'd have a day of fun in the sun. "We're going to play all day," he'd said to her.

A thrill ran up her spine. Kevin was proving to her again and again that he wasn't the same man she'd set out to divorce. He'd learned how to delegate. He'd learned how to have fun. He'd learned that there was more to life than work. Cara smiled as she showered and pulled on a breezy, flowered sundress.

When Alicia Montoya called, Cara couldn't refuse to meet her for coffee. Clearly upset, Alicia needed a friend. Half an hour later, they sat on tufted sofa chairs drinking espresso at a local coffee shop near Cara's hotel.

"Thanks for meeting me on such short notice," Alicia said, her pretty face forlorn. Dressed in black, as if in mourning, she wore her hair pulled tightly back, held by a clasp. Light pink lipstick brought color to her olive skin tones.

Alicia played with the rim of her coffee mug, searching for the right words. "This is…hard."

"I know," Cara said, compassion filling her heart. Alicia wanted so much to be accepted. It couldn't be easy being Alejandro Montoya's sister. Alicia had been on cloud nine last night when they'd last spoken. She'd been so happy that she'd met Rick Jones and he'd asked her out. Cara still didn't know who Rick was, but judging by the look on Alicia's face last night, he'd made her very happy. Then there had been the blowup outside of the club and poor Alicia had looked panic stricken. "I'm glad you called me."

"Are you? I think I'm putting you in the middle."

Cara reached for her arm. "No, I'm not in the middle of anything. You're my friend."

Alicia lowered her stiff shoulders and let go a sigh. "Oh, Cara. I can't tell you what that means to me."

"It means a lot to me, too."

"It's just that everyone thinks the worst of my brother."

"I can't pretend I don't know that. Alex and Lance go way back and none of it is pretty."

"Your husband doesn't like him either."

"Kevin thinks Alex blocked one of his projects. It's business more than a personal thing."

Alicia nodded her understanding, her expression somber. "Alex didn't break up the reception last night. He wouldn't do that."

"Are you certain?"

"Yes. I'm sure. I was with him all night, except for the time I met you in the ladies' room. He never complained about the reception. In fact, he didn't know about it until I mentioned it to him."

"But you said you'd heard the music playing."

"Alex barely noticed it and it certainly didn't

bother us. He may think Lance a rival, but he's not that petty. I just know in my heart Alex would never do something like that."

No, Cara thought. If only Alicia knew what bigger crimes the Brody brothers accused him of perpetrating, she'd be devastated. "Alicia, I believe you. But Lance and Alex are going to have to find a way to work out their differences on their own."

"My brother isn't perfect. He's stubborn and prideful, but he's a good man. It hurt to see him being accused last night in front of so many people. It's a good thing Kevin intervened."

"Yes, I agree. Lance looked ready for a fight."

"And Alex never backs down from one."

Cara smiled at her friend with sadness in her heart. "Not a good combination, I'm afraid." She didn't have any answers but she knew Alicia didn't expect any. She only needed a friend to talk to.

"I'm glad we spoke."

"Me, too. I hope it helped a little."

"It did." Alicia sipped her espresso, which up until this point had gone untouched. "Oh, this is good."

Cara sipped her decaf. "So what are you doing the rest of the day?"

A smile broke out on her face. "Well, I think they're having a sale at Sweet Nothings today."

"You're going back for that pink baby-doll lingerie!"

"I think so. Just in case, mind you. It's nice to know there's hope of wearing it one day."

Cara's laugh displayed her great delight. "That a girl."

"What about you? Do you have plans for the rest of the day?"

Cara nodded with thoughts of Kevin's deep-blue eyes on her as he'd bid her good-night. "I have plans with Kevin later today."

Alicia took her hand and gazed directly into her eyes. "I hope it works out for you and Kevin, Cara. You deserve to be happy."

Cara couldn't agree more. She wanted to be happy again. "Thank you. And remember, I'm here if you need me."

At precisely 1:00 p.m., Kevin picked Cara up in front of her hotel. He opened the car door for her, took her tote bag and tossed it into the trunk. "What's in the bag?"

"Everything necessary for fun in the sun," she quipped. "Bathing suit, sunscreen, oils and lotions."

Kevin shot her a heated glance from the driver's seat. He looked simply edible in tan trousers and a black polo shirt sitting behind the wheel of his powerful sports car. "Sounds perfect."

He gunned the car and they took off toward Somerset. "Are we going to the club?" she asked.

"No way. I have something better in mind." He swiveled his head to gaze at her once again. "You look beautiful, Cara."

So do you, she didn't add. Her heart sang. "Thanks."

Kevin reached over to take her hand as he drove on, his fingers wrapping around hers with gentle possession. Cara closed her eyes briefly. Electricity flowed between them. She felt it and knew that what they had was more than simple physical attraction.

Kevin pulled up in front of a large, lovely cottage-like home on the outskirts of Somerset. Cobblestone and a white picket fence marked the entry, the garden robust with colorful pansies in full bloom and sculpted greenery.

Cara stared at the home, then questioned Kevin with a curious look.

"It's a rental I own. Vacant at the moment and ours for the day."

"How convenient," she teased.

"Isn't it though?"

Kevin opened the car door for her and lifted her tote bag from the trunk easily, laying it onto her shoulder. With a hand to her back, he guided her down the cobblestone path to the front door. Fidgeting with a set of keys, he finally came up with the one that fit in the lock. "Here it is."

"Good, because breaking and entering won't look good on my record."

Kevin kissed her smack on the lips. "Sassy today."

"Always."

"That's what I love about you."

The minute the words were out, she knew Kevin wished he hadn't spoken them. He turned away from her quickly and fumbled with the key. After a few seconds, he managed to get the door open. "Sticky lock," he explained with a little hitch in his throat.

Cara remained silent.

He guided her into the house, which had a country feel to it. From what she could see, the entry hall led to a massive living space, complete with a ceiling-to-floor stone fireplace, wood beams above and large windows on either side of an oak-framed set of French doors.

"Very nice. How long has it been empty?"

"A month. The previous tenants moved to Europe. The new tenants move in next week. It's been cleaned and polished to a shine."

"I can see that." Cara stared at the shiny wood floors beneath her feet and imagined dancing on them. "The rooms are big, but it still feels cozy to me."

"Looks even better with furniture."

Kevin tugged on the tote bag hanging from her shoulder. "C'mon. I want to show you the grounds."

Kevin opened the French doors wide and led her out to a large stone patio. Three sets of love seats wrapped around an in-ground fire pit. Kevin took her hand and led her down a small staircase to the private garden below, infused with bright color.

"Beautiful," Cara murmured.

A swimming pool the size of a small lake came into view beyond a low outcropping of dark green hedges.

Kevin gestured to a mini-replica of the cottage serving as the pool house. "Two pitchers of marga-ritas are waiting for us in there, one strawberry."

Cara peered into his eyes. "You thought of every-thing."

Kevin grinned. "That remains to be seen."

Cara walked along the path to the black-bottom pool. Kicking her sandals off, she dipped her toes in. "You did think of everything. It's the perfect tem-perature for me."

"Well, then, let's take a dip."

"But where's your stuff?" she asked, noting that he hadn't brought a beach bag for himself.

"Don't need anything." He sat down in the center of a slatted lounge chair and took off his shoes.

He didn't need anything?

Cara's heart raced.

Next, he stood and removed his shirt, pulling the polo over his head in one fluid move. Texas sunshine streamed down on his bare chest. Ripped with muscle and bronzed as a golden statue, Kevin took her breath away. When he unzipped his trousers, she took a deep gulp of oxygen, unable to avert her gaze. "Kevin?"

He pulled down his trousers and stepped out of them, his swim trunks appearing underneath.

"What's taking you so long?" He gestured with a nod of his head. "The pool house has a dressing area."

"R-right," she said, taking hold of her senses. "I'll be back in a sec." Just before she entered the dressing room, she heard a splash from Kevin's dive into the pool.

After donning her two-piece, strawberry-red bathing suit, she grabbed two plush white towels and hugged them to her chest. Feeling foolishly self-conscious at the amount of skin showing, Cara glanced in the mirror and wondered what had possessed her to buy this skimpy suit.

She'd never worn it in public before. And granted, being poolside with her husband wasn't exactly like being on the sands of Waikiki in the middle of summer, yet she still felt terribly exposed.

"Cara, you coming?" Kevin's boyish tone brought a smile to her lips. "I'm getting lonely out here."

She glanced at the refrigerator in the small kitchenette on the way out. "You want a margarita?" she called.

"Later, babe."

Cara nibbled on her lip and exited the pool house just as Kevin glided out of the water, his head lifting and his gaze zeroing in on her. Water sloshed off his shoulders as he rose to stand in the pool. He swiped back his short hair and smiled, reaching for her. "Drop the towels, Cara."

She let them fall from her hands near the edge of the pool. "Don't pull me in."

He secured her hand in his. "I won't. Take your time, babe. I could stand here all day and look at you."

Heat crawled up her neck from the soft tone of his voice and the captivating way his gaze stayed on her. Slowly, she lowered her body down to sit on the edge of the pool. Putting her feet in, she wiggled her toes. "Feels good."

Kevin ran his hands along her thighs, moistening her legs with pool water. "Yeah, it does."

"I don't just jump into things anymore," she explained.

"You used to." Kevin's deliberate touch along her thighs made her bones melt.

"I've changed." She was more mature, more thoughtful about things. She'd learned a valuable lesson being married to Kevin. She hadn't really known him when they'd married. His drive and ambition had caught her off guard. She vowed not to let her emotions dictate her future anymore. Every single decision she'd made since leaving Somerset had been done with great thought and deliberation.

"I have, too."

Cara stared at Kevin. He had changed. He'd proven that over the past two weeks. But she didn't know if she could trust in that. Or in him anymore.

But she did love him.

That fact couldn't be denied.

Kevin parted her legs and grabbed her around the waist. "Whenever you're ready."

She nodded. She was ready to take a chance. She wrapped her legs around his waist and her arms around his neck. He lowered her gently into the water, swirling her around and around, slowly, their eyes never parting.

Buoyant and floating, Cara felt a wave of peace and happiness she hadn't experienced in a long time. She reached out to touch his face, the stubble of his day-old beard grazing her fingers. Then she leaned in and kissed him softly on the mouth.

Kevin stopped and cast her a long, penetrating look, his eyes searching hers intently. Tingles ran up and down her body. Her throat dry, powerful emotions swept over her.

"Cara?"

Cara pressed her fingers to his lips. "Shh, don't say anything, sweetheart."

She couldn't bear to hear what he had to say. She didn't want the mood to turn serious or change in any way. It had been so long since she'd felt such serenity. She wanted to live in the moment and not analyze every word Kevin spoke or scrutinize every gesture he made. "Fun in the sun, remember?" She kissed him again.

Pleased, he groaned deep and waded through the water with her in his arms until they reached the wall of the pool. Resting his back on the tile, he tugged her closer, her breasts rising above the water to press against his chest.

Kevin kissed her fiercely, his mouth traveling over her face, her chin, her throat and shoulders, nipping at her skin and creating impossible tingles that spun her mind in ten different directions.

"Did I tell you how much I like your bathing suit?"

Cara kissed his shoulder. "You neglected to say that earlier."

He cupped her rear end, his fingers spread over her cheeks. "I do. I like it a lot. What there is of it."

"Oh, yeah?" She wiggled out of his arms and dived into the water, swimming a few laps from width to width. Things were heating up too fast between her and Kevin. As much as she wanted him, she had an impending need to protect herself.

When she came up out of the water after her swim, she faced Kevin from across the shallow end of the pool. "I'm ready for a margarita."

"I'll get them," he said without hesitation and she watched him lift himself out of the water and head to the pool house.

Kevin poured Cara a strawberry margarita, then rimmed his glass with salt and poured himself one from the other pitcher. Putting the pitchers back in the refrigerator, he lifted out two covered plates—lunch. He'd had a chef from his favorite restaurant prepare gourmet sandwiches and salad, and had them delivered here, refusing the chef's offer to serve the meal. Kevin wanted to be completely alone with Cara today.

They had two days left together.

He winced, thinking his days were numbered in regard to her. Soon, he'd be a free man, his plan accomplished and revenge complete.

He hadn't expected to regret his decision, though. He'd become accustomed to having Cara by his side again. Yet it was her decision to come to Somerset for a divorce. She hadn't wanted reconciliation and if he hadn't blackmailed her into seeing him these past two weeks, she would have been long gone, signed divorce papers in hand. He couldn't get over that. She'd rejected him not once but twice in his life.

His ego had taken a pounding and his pride was at stake. On many levels, he wished he hadn't come up with his brilliant scheme for payback. Because he, too, had suffered the consequences of spending time with Cara and wanting her with a need so great, he'd had trouble keeping to his plan, again and again.

Kevin set the dishes on a tray along with the margaritas and hesitated before bringing them outside.

Why not give in to his needs now? Why not seduce her today and be done with it? They'd been leading up to this point since the moment she'd agreed to his plan. Why wait? Why extend the torturous need they had for each other?

Kevin debated that notion as he picked up the tray and carried it outside. He found Cara in a chaise lounge, sliding sunscreen oil onto her legs. He stopped to take in the scene, watching her finish coating her legs with the golden liquid. Once she was done with her legs, she spread the oil onto her torso, working it in and then farther up, onto her chest. She grazed over the swells of her breasts with the oil and slid her fingers slightly underneath her swimsuit top, making sure to cover every inch of exposed skin.

"You should have let me do that," Kevin said, making light of the extremely sexy scene he'd just witnessed.

"You were taking too long, buster. A girl's got to protect herself, you know?"

Kevin set the tray down on a glass table between her lounge and his. He gazed at her very appealing chest for a few lingering seconds. "Hungry?"

"Famished," she said. "Swimming gives me an appetite."

He liked that about Cara. She wasn't one to not eat when hungry. Usually, she scarfed up her food with enthusiasm.

He handed her the margarita. "To…us."

She gazed at him, puzzled. He picked up his glass and touched it to hers. "To us," she finally replied with a small smile.

They conversed while eating lunch and sipping margaritas in the sunshine. Cara told stories of her dance students, some of whom had gone on to real careers in dance and other lonely souls who'd pay the fee just to have some one-on-one attention from a pretty dance instructor. Kevin enjoyed listening to her—the animation in her voice and her broad gestures spoke of her love and commitment to her business. When she'd first arrived, he'd resented hearing of her success, but now he felt proud of what she'd accomplished.

"You know," she said in a thoughtful tone, "I think Somerset might need a dance studio."

Kevin stopped chewing for a second. He gazed into Cara's bright eyes. Finally swallowing, he asked, "Here?"

"Why not? I like it here. I could expand my horizons in this direction as well as any."

Kevin didn't reply. It was one thing being divorced from Cara while she was miles away, but having her come back here as a single woman? He didn't know if he was ready for that. Visions of bumping into her while she was on a date with another man, or seeing her with his friends, didn't sit well with him. A dozen emotions swirled in his gut. He felt sick to his stomach at the prospect.

When his silence became obvious, Cara asked, "Kevin, would you have a problem with that?"

Hell, yeah. "No, not at all," he lied, hoping the idea was just a passing fancy.

Cara watched him carefully, then lowered her lashes. "It's just a thought." She sipped her margarita and shrugged. He couldn't help but feel he'd disappointed her somehow, though.

Shoving the notion from his head, he was determined to enjoy the day with Cara without worry. They went on to more amiable topics of discussion as they finished their lunch.

Cara sighed and leaned back in her chaise lounge, lifting her face to the sun. "This is really nice, Kevin. I'm glad you invited me here."

"Don't get too comfortable, baby. You still have to do me."

Cara lifted partly up from the lounge and peered at him. "What?"

He pointed to the sunscreen oil. Then grinned.

Cara shook her head, a wide smile erupting on her face. "Funny, Kevin."

"Well?"

"Okay, lie back." Kevin obeyed without hesitation. Cara poured oil onto her hands and straddled his legs.

He looked up into her pretty sky-blue eyes, barely able to contain his lust. When she touched him, her hands splaying across his chest, he groaned inwardly. She massaged the oil in, her fingertips light, gliding over his skin. He watched her as she leaned forward, intent on her task, her beautiful cleavage in full view and practically begging for his touch. It took every ounce of his willpower not to pull her down on top of him and show her what she did to him.

Once she'd massaged his arms and shoulders, he took the bottle out of her hand. "I think you've done enough."

"You don't sound grateful," she said, her teasing tone too much to take.

"Oh, I'm very grateful," he said, wrapping his arms around her neck and pulling her close. "You know, it's very private here. No one can see what we're doing."

Her eyes went wide with surprise. With that, he pulled her closer and crushed his lips to hers, absorbing every inch of her. But it wasn't nearly enough. He parted her lips and drove his tongue into her mouth, tasting the sweetness of strawberries and her unabashed passion.

In just a few seconds, Kevin had Cara sprawled atop him, his erection straining the confines of his swim trunks. She fit him perfectly and made him crazy with want. He untied her top easily, one little slice of material keeping him from heaven. Her breasts spilled out and Kevin caressed them, holding their weight in his hands, flicking his thumb over both tips until they pebbled into beautiful erect buds.

His gaze trained on hers, he took one perfect globe into his mouth. Cara's eyes slowly closed and a beautiful expression flowed over her features.

He suckled her until both buds were moistened and glowed in the warming sunshine.

Kevin wrapped his hands around her bottom and positioned her onto his erection until she felt the full force of his desire. "I can't wait to have you."

Cara moaned and kissed him fiercely, her breasts crushing his chest. In another second, they'd both be beyond reason. But Kevin held back. This wasn't in his plan. He wanted a full night with Cara, under his own terms. He had it all set in his mind.

Yet he wouldn't deny them both this moment of pleasure. He dipped his hand under her swimsuit and touched her sweetly sensitive spot. "Feel good?" he whispered.

Beyond words, Cara nodded, her lids half-closed. Kevin stroked her carefully with deliberate movements, laying his fingers along the soft folds of her sex.

Wrapping his other hand around her curly blond locks, he pulled her head down to his and kissed her over and over again, her body rocking back and forth, finding a sensual rhythm.

"Oh, Kevin," Cara whimpered, as he continued to glide his fingers over her folds. Kevin watched as tension built quickly, her body rocking forcefully, an expression of sheer lust crossing her beautiful face.

His heart ached witnessing her sheer abandon as her breathing escalated and her body tightened. He stroked her harder, deeper and longer. She arched up and her release came in powerful short bursts of exquisite movements. Watching her orgasm stole his breath.

And made him rethink his plan.

Once spent, a satisfied sigh escaped her throat and she laid her head on his chest. He massaged her lower back, holding her loosely in his arms. "Damn."

"Yeah, damn," she repeated.

Thoughts of making love to Cara on the lounge chair entered his head. Hell, he was ready and Cara wasn't denying him. But once they made love, he'd have to make good on his deal to deliver signed divorce papers.

She wants out of our marriage.

This is the price she's willing to pay.

And I'm paying for it, too, a little annoying voice inside his head reminded him.

"You know what we both need?"

Cara chuckled, the sound emanating from deep in her throat. "Oh, yeah. I know."

Kevin laid one last kiss onto her lips. "Good, then come with me."

Kevin lifted her up and in one sweeping movement, he jumped into the pool, taking Cara with him.

Ten

Cara lay in bed the next morning with thoughts of Kevin intruding on her sleep. Visions of their day together raced through her mind.

Fun in the sun.

Yes, Kevin had seen to that. And much more. Her body still sated from the incredible climax he'd provided her, Cara relived every exquisite moment of his unselfish sexual advance. She was completely, one hundred percent in love with him and had come close to telling him ten times yesterday by the pool.

But Kevin had never spoken of the future to her. He'd never once let on that he wanted reconciliation. He'd held back his own desire yesterday in order to keep his blackmail deal with her.

Why?

Had nothing changed between them over these past two weeks?

Lance's comments about Kevin hurting her were never far from her mind. What had he meant? She couldn't help but think Lance, even in his intoxicated state—or maybe because of it—had set out to warn her about Kevin.

And then at the pool, when she had mentioned her plan to open a dance studio in Somerset, Kevin's nonreaction had stung her pride. He hadn't said much about it, until she had pressed him for an answer. He'd given her a halfhearted reply. It had been clear that Kevin didn't like the idea.

In fact, for a few seconds, his whole demeanor had changed. She hadn't dwelled on his reaction yesterday—they'd been too wrapped up in each other for her to have entertained clear thoughts. But now, in the clarity of morning, she faced facts.

"He doesn't want me in Somerset," Cara muttered, her heart hurting with that realization.

Cara mustered her courage. Instead of deliberating about it all day, driving herself crazy, she made up her mind to find out the truth.

Or at least find out what Lance's comments had meant.

With that notion in mind, Cara rose from bed and showered. She dried her hair and put on a bright canary-yellow sundress, slipped her feet into sandals, then grabbed her cell phone from her purse and dialed Lance's number.

An hour later, she faced Lance Brody in his high-rise executive office at Brody Oil and Gas. "Thanks for seeing me on short notice," Cara said, taking one of two seats facing his desk.

"My pleasure," he said, sitting casually on the edge of his desk, just a few feet from her. "Would you like a cup of coffee, breakfast, anything?" Lance leaned over his desk, with a finger on the intercom button, ready to accommodate her.

"No thanks, Lance."

He straightened and smiled. "Okay." His dark eyes searching, he wore an earnest expression. "I was a little surprised that you asked to see me. What's up?"

Cara straightened the folds of her dress, then looked deep into his eyes. "It's about Kevin."

"O-kay," Lance said slowly, looking a little confused.

"The other night at your house, you said something to me that I didn't understand."

Lance tossed his head back with self-deprecating laughter. "I probably said a lot of things that didn't make sense that night."

"You made a point of taking me aside and warning me about Kevin. You said he was hard-headed. That he would hurt me."

Lance averted his gaze. He found the floor inter-esting, then the wall. "Did I?"

"Do you remember saying that to me?"

Lance shot her a direct look. "No, I don't remember saying that."

"But you do know what that means, don't you?"

Lance rose, walked behind his desk, then faced her again.

"Cara," he said, taking a deep breath. He rubbed the back of his neck. "If I said something to upset you that night, I apologize."

Cara shook her head and stood. "The only thing that's upsetting me is not knowing what you meant. You know what's going on with Kevin. Now, are you going to tell me the truth?"

Lance stared at her for a few long seconds. She could almost see the debate going on in his head. He *knew* something. She pinned him with a penetrating gaze, refusing to back down—even if it meant hearing something about Kevin that she didn't want to hear.

"He's one of my best friends," Lance said.

Cara stood her ground, patiently. She wouldn't let Lance off the hook. She continued to stare.

"Okay," he said with reluctance. "Have a seat. It's probably better this way. You two need to talk this through. I'll tell you what I know."

Cara glanced at the clock radio on the hotel's night table. Kevin would be here any second. It would be their last night together and she planned on making it memorable.

She'd had to pull the words out of Lance's mouth earlier today. Poor man. He'd tried hard not to hurt her, but it hadn't taken too many words to make Cara see the whole picture. She'd always been great with putting puzzle pieces together, making them fit. And once she'd gotten the corners of Lance's knowledge assembled, she'd put the entire puzzle together very quickly.

She knew Kevin's plan and was through playing his game. It was high time she took control of the situation. Tonight, she'd play her own game and sadly, no one would come out the winner.

Furious with her soon-to-be ex, Cara hadn't had time to feel the tremendous hurt she knew would follow. Right now, fury fueled her to give Kevin a dose of his own medicine.

"You deserve it, *sweetheart*."

When the knock sounded on her hotel door, Cara assumed the guise both mentally and physically. She tossed her arms into her silk robe and walked over to the door.

Taking a deep breath first, steadying her nerves, she opened the door.

Kevin stood in the doorway, wearing a very expensive dark Italian suit. Groomed to perfection, there was no denying his sexual appeal and charisma. Cara's heart lurched, but she ignored the pangs.

His expression dropped, seeing her in her robe. "Hi. Am I early?"

Cara shook her head. "No, you're right on time."

Kevin's brows furrowed, puzzled. "I'll tell the limo driver to wait. Dinner's not until eight. I have a great night planned—"

Cara dropped the robe, letting it puddle at her feet. She took great satisfaction seeing Kevin's deep-blue eyes widen with appreciation. She allowed him a few seconds of shock, seeing her dressed in the one-piece formfitting black-lace unitard. Strategically placed lace was meant to tease and tempt, exposed skin in erogenous zones that would make Catwoman blush.

Cara grabbed Kevin by his sleek silk tie and yanked him inside the room. Extending her leg past him in a fluid lift, she kicked the door shut and pinned him against it. "No date, no dinner. It's time, Kevin. For us."

Cara wrapped her arms around his neck and crushed her mouth to his, leaving the taste of wild cherry on his lips.

She backed away and stared at him. Thoroughly confused, Kevin glanced around the hotel room. Two dozen pillar candles lit the room and flavored the air with a sweet vanilla scent. Rose petals decorated her king-size bed, the sheets turned down provocatively. Chocolate-covered strawberries and a champagne bottle chilling in a silver bucket stood on a tray by the window table.

Kevin leaned back, thumping his head against the wall. "Cara, what is all this?"

She smiled. "You talk too much, baby." She loosened his tie and lifted it over his head. "The time for talking is over. Make love to me. It's what we both want."

Kevin blinked, then stared into her eyes. Cara

kept the ruse up—she wouldn't deny herself this night. As long as she was in control, she'd be fine. She unbuttoned his shirt and ran her hands along his hard, perfect chest. "C'mon, babe. I thought you'd be as hot for this as I am."

Cara nipped at his lower lip, then rimmed his mouth with her tongue. Kevin groaned and slipped his tongue into her mouth, taking her on a wild erotic ride with just that one frenzied kiss.

"Mmm, Kevin," she said, licking her lips, pulling away from him just a bit. "I can't wait for you to be inside me."

Kevin groaned deeper and pulled her close, so that every juncture of their bodies touched. Exquisite tingles ran up and down her length, his manhood already evident. "Damn it, Cara. Keep talking that way, and we won't make it over to that bed."

She tossed her head back, a throaty laugh escaping. "Since when did we *ever* need a bed?"

Cara nipped at his lips again. Kevin heaved a breath and pulled off his shirt. Immediately, Cara touched him again, running her palms over his skin, pressing her tongue to his erect nipples.

Kevin lifted her easily and started for the bed. "I'm older now. I like creature comforts."

Cara shook her head, gazing into his eyes. "Oh, that's a shame. I wanted to dance for you."

Kevin stopped in midstride. He peered down at her with inquisitive eyes, his voice filled with keen interest. "Dance for me?"

She nodded innocently.

"What do you want me to do?"

"Just lie down on the bed and watch."

Kevin sucked oxygen into his chest. "Okay."

He set her down. Cara put her iPod in the dock on the nightstand and hit Play, selecting a specific song. When she turned around, Kevin was bathed in candlelight, lying on his back on the bed, his head propped up on her pillow.

"You are a beautiful woman, Cara Novak," Kevin said in a humble tone.

Cara closed her eyes and felt the music fill her. Then she began to move, swaying her body, her hips gyrating sensually. Everything she had inside, everything she felt for Kevin, the love she'd never declared, came out in the dance.

She gave Kevin this gift, this exposing of her innermost being, so that he would never forget her. So that he would look upon this time with her and know that no other woman could provide what she had given to him.

She danced, flowing to the music, lost in her own movements, giving to Kevin what she'd never given another man.

Cara didn't have a vengeful bone in her body, yet this she felt compelled to do. For her own sense of justice. He'd hurt her beyond belief and she hoped this gift would be his undoing. She danced and danced, her eyes half-lidded, her body in seamless motion with the music and her spirit free.

When the song ended, Cara opened her eyes fully, facing Kevin. The awed expression on his face nearly caved her resolve. "Cara," he said, opening his mouth to speak. He couldn't find the words and Cara knew at that moment what Kevin felt was genuine and true.

She smiled and for a few seconds she forgot his deceit.

"I'm not through."

She chose a different song. It was smooth and sensual, filled with lyrics about suspicions. She moved slowly, erotically, peeling herself out of her lacy one-piece. She stepped out of the garment and stood before Kevin, naked. "Touch me, Kevin. I want to remember your hands on me."

"Cara," Kevin said, his voice little more than a croak. He came to her on his knees and helped her onto the bed. On her knees, too, they faced each other. Kevin kissed her, then touched his fingers to her lips. He moved his hand down her throat and kissed her there, then lower. He cupped her breasts in his hands, circling them and making Cara's nerves go absolutely raw.

She closed her eyes and hung on to him, relishing the feel of his hands caressing her. He skimmed his hands down her torso, teasing, tempting, then cupped her womanhood gently, his fingers lingering just enough to make her head swim.

Next, he touched her thighs as far as he could

reach and wound his hands around her legs to the back. Her skin prickled in anticipation and when he touched the rounds of her buttocks, she let go a pleasured moan.

Kevin took hold of her head then, his restraint nearly spent. He crushed his lips to hers, again and again. "You're killing me slowly, babe."

Tension wound in her belly. She needed Kevin. She needed to make this memory, before she bid him goodbye for good. Taking the reins, she shoved at his chest, pushing him down on the bed. He went willingly with a big smile on his face.

She undid his belt and pulled it free of the loops. Next she took off his shoes and socks, tossing them aside before removing his slacks. He lay naked before her now, his thick erection a temptation all in itself. Cara cupped him, wrapping her hand around his silken shaft. She stroked him several times, eliciting curses from deep in his throat. "Babe?"

"I know what I'm doing, Kevin."

"Ah...uh, no doubt, but—"

Cara replaced her hand with her mouth, taking Kevin inside and silencing any complaints he may have had. He lay back quietly while she made love to him that way.

Tension built quickly from there. Their breathing heaved hard and they moved with a need that could only be satisfied one way. Scalding heat and sticky moisture fused their bodies. Cara wanted this. She'd dreamed of this. And she wouldn't be denied.

She rose atop Kevin, straddling his legs, and peered deep into his eyes. He seemed to understand her need. He reached for her hips and she lowered down on him, taking him inside her. Sensations ripped through her system, pleasure and desire, need and want, fulfillment and appreciation. Cara cried out. Kevin groaned as if in pain. She looked into his eyes, joined with him now, complete. Vivid memories of earth-shattering sex and dire love crossed between them.

"Oh, yes, Cara."

"I know, babe."

She moved down farther and he let go a grunt of satisfaction. She rose up and then took him in even deeper. Her skin prickled. Her body tightened around him. Her nipples budded to round peaks.

They peered at each other amid candlelight and rose petals. But none of that mattered anymore. Their sheer joining was enough to warrant erotic images and romantic atmosphere. It was all that either of them needed.

With Kevin's guidance, Cara moved on him, riding him up and down, each time taking him deeper, fuller, faster until Cara's body grew tight with climactic tension. Hot currents shocked her nerve endings and she rose up.

"Let go, baby," Kevin whispered, his voice strained.

She slammed down on him, as small rockets of sensation whipped through her. She moved back and forth, her body tight, her nerves sensitized. Her release exploded hard and fast and shook her to her core.

She reveled in the sensation a moment, before Kevin reached for her, bringing her down onto his hot body. "That was amazing," he said, between kisses.

"Now it's your turn," Cara said, kissing him fiercely.

"Oh, yeah."

Kevin rolled her onto her back and placed little kisses along her face, jaw, chin and throat. He cupped her breast and paid a good deal of attention to the erect bud with his tongue.

His thick erection still unfulfilled, Cara squirmed under him. "Hurry, baby. I need you inside me again."

"Just making sure you're ready."

"I'm always ready."

Kevin kissed her one last time, before spreading her legs and entering her, driving deep in one thrust. "I love that about you."

Cara felt as if she'd come home. Being with Kevin, making love, sharing intimacies, all seemed so right. There were so many things Kevin said he loved about her…yet he didn't love her at all. Sadness filled her heart again, knowing that this was all a vengeful little game. Only tonight, she'd made up the rules.

Soon, it would all be over.

Cara pushed those thoughts away and focused on the pleasure Kevin brought her. She vowed to make him remember this night and nothing would stop her.

Kevin sustained slow, fulfilling thrusts long enough to arouse Cara to the peak of orgasm again. He moved on her as if committing her to memory, every powerful drive of his body deliberate and controlled. "Cara, I've missed you."

Cara blocked that from her mind. She refused to believe him and passed it off as ramblings from a sexually aroused lover. Instead she focused on the wonderful little explosions occurring in her body.

When Kevin arched, his face given to release, Cara rose up, those tiny explosions waiting, building. Kevin called out her name, driving one last force into her body and Cara let go. The orgasm rocked them both, each lifting, releasing, the complete, agonizing pleasure of their bodies aligning and bursting as one.

Kevin came down on Cara gently, taking her in his arms. He kissed her passionately, murmuring, "I knew it would be like this."

Cara smiled sadly. The truth was the truth. "Me, too."

Cara woke up to an empty bed. The room bathed in candlelight, she squinted and focused her eyes as she sat straight up in bed. Kevin stood across the room, his slacks on, his feet bare, pouring two flutes of champagne. "Nice nap?" he asked, turning to her.

"Mmm." They'd exhausted each other, making love again, christening several corners of the room both in standing and sitting positions. After, they'd both fallen into a deep, if short, slumber.

"It's time for champagne, babe."

Cara looked at the digital clock on the nightstand, then rose and pulled on her robe. She tightened the belt with a tug and approached him. "To toast our divorce?"

Kevin visibly winced.

Cara gathered her fury. "Or maybe you'd like to extract another ten or twenty minutes out of my soul?"

"Cara, what's wrong?" He attempted to hand the flute to her, but she wouldn't take it. She refused to take anything from Kevin, ever again.

Cara walked over to the nightstand and opened the drawer. "I think I've met all the terms of your blackmail, Kevin." She pulled out the divorce papers. "Now it's time for you to sign on the dotted line."

A tic worked in Kevin's jaw. He eyed her carefully and set down the champagne flutes.

"It's almost midnight. My two weeks are over." Cara rolled her eyes dramatically. "Thank God."

Kevin's face flushed with color. He strode over to her and grabbed both of her arms. "What's gotten into you?"

"Besides you?"

Kevin flinched as though he'd been slapped.

"I want my divorce, Kevin. I've earned it." Cara's voice wobbled as she mustered her courage. She refused to cry, to let Kevin see his victory.

He'd wanted to hurt her and he had. She'd taken the bait, hook, line and sinker. She'd fallen in love with him, but she wouldn't give him the satisfaction of knowing that he'd won his little game.

"I don't believe you."

Oh, how she hated him.

"Why? Why don't you believe me? Because I played along and let you manipulate me the entire time I was here? Did you think I'd fall head over heels in love with you again?"

Cara walked away from him, picked up a glass of champagne and downed it in one giant gulp. She turned her back on him. "Sign them and leave, Kevin."

"You're angry, Cara. Damn it, so was I. When you left me. I couldn't believe you walked out on our marriage. Was it so easy for you? You just picked up and started a new life in Dallas."

She whirled around. "That's not what this is about, Kevin. Not at all. I thought you'd changed, but you've proven that you haven't. You're still out for blood, to win at all costs, no matter who gets hurt. You had to have your revenge, didn't you? You had to break me. You had to—"

"Who told you that?" Kevin approached her, his gaze piercing. "Where did you hear that?"

"Don't deny it. I know it's true."

Kevin sucked oxygen in and shook his head. "Damn it, Cara. Damn it all."

Cara downed the second glass of champagne, then turned her back on him once and for all. Her heart ached just looking at him, thinking of the passion they'd just shared. Not once had he apologized. Not once had he offered any sign of hope. Not once had he confessed to wanting reconciliation. The ache went deep, slicing through her gut. Her body shook painfully and tears welled in her eyes. "Sign the papers, Kevin. Then get out."

"Fine," he said. She didn't dare look at him. She didn't dare turn around. She waited, with her back to him, listening as he picked up his clothes and slammed the door shut behind him.

Then Cara fell apart. Tears streamed down her face and she sobbed in painful shudders. She felt as if she'd been broken in half. Her head ached and her heart plummeted to deep depths of despair.

Her marriage was over. She made her way to the bed and lowered down, shaking and seeking the bed frame for support. Braving a glance at the nightstand to see the signed evidence of her broken vows, she blinked. "What?"

Catching her breath, she got up and gave the nightstand a better look. With a quick tug, she opened the drawer and myriad thoughts flooded her head.

The divorce papers were gone.

Kevin slammed his penthouse door and tossed his jacket aside. Ten bouquets set about the room scented the air with sweetness. Candles stood at the ready in every corner of the penthouse, waiting to be lit. Decadent finger desserts arranged on the dining-room table added to the ambience, as champagne chilled in the wine closet. The seduction scene he'd planned mocked him with sickening clarity.

Cara had beaten him in his own game. She'd been cunning and clever and sexier than any woman he'd ever known. She'd fooled him and he hadn't seen it coming.

Yet he'd accomplished his goals and hated himself for it. Everything they'd built upon during the past two weeks had been wiped out in just a few minutes tonight. Kevin had thought he knew what he wanted. Apparently, he'd been wrong. Unmindful of the time, he picked up his cell phone and dialed Darius, waking him.

"Hey, man, do you know what time it is?"

"Yeah, sorry. Listen, I need to know if you spoke with Cara today."

"No, I didn't speak with Cara. Aren't your two weeks up yet?"

"As of about an hour ago, yeah. My time's up. Gotta run."

Next, he dialed Lance's number. "Did you see Cara today?"

Lance hesitated before answering. "Yeah, Cara came to see me today. She knew something was up with you and she asked me for honesty."

"What did you tell her?"

"I didn't have to tell her too much. She's an intelligent woman. She figured out what you were doing. You should have seen the look on her face."

"Mad as hell, I assume?"

"No, that would have been easier to take. More like complete devastation. She looked defeated and hurt. She's in love with you."

Kevin squeezed his eyes shut. He'd seen the devastation on her face tonight, heard it in her quivering voice. He'd wanted to go to her and tell her truths he'd only just realized, but she'd been too angry and too hurt. She wouldn't have listened to him. She wouldn't have believed him. He'd needed to regroup and figure some things out. "I blew it with her. And don't tell me, 'I told you so.'"

Lance sighed into the receiver. "Did you sign the divorce papers?"

"No. It's the first time I've ever reneged on a deal. But I couldn't sign them. I took them with me."

"Do you love her, Kev?"

"Yeah, I just realized it tonight. I've never stopped loving her. But telling her wouldn't have meant anything to her. Not after the hell I put her through."

"Now what?"

"Now I'm going to have to blackmail her one more time, to get her to listen to me."

"Oh, man. Good luck."

The divorce papers are signed. You just have to come pick them up.

Cara fumed as she drove her rental car to the address Kevin had given her. He'd called this morning, offering a limo service to take her to the destination. But Cara had refused. She didn't want anything to do with Kevin Novak, his limo or his life. From now on, she could only count on herself.

"Why is everything with you so difficult, Kevin?" she muttered as she drove into Somerset. "Couldn't you have just signed the papers last night? No, you have to do everything on your own terms. You always have to be in control."

Cara cursed as she sped along, looking at the address Kevin had given her. She had just enough time to pick up her divorce papers and get to the airport. Her flight left in two hours.

She pulled into a newly built mini-mall in an upscale location of Somerset and double-checked the address. She was in the right place. She parked the car and took a deep breath, then got out and strode into a building still under construction.

She found herself standing in the center of a large, empty shell of a space, sawdust on the floor and windows yet to be installed. Kevin came out of the shadows to face her. For what it was worth, he looked as awful as she felt, his eyes red, his face troubled. Wearing the same clothes he'd worn last night, he appeared rumpled.

"Hello, Cara."

Cara drew a steadying breath. "Did you bring the papers?"

He nodded and gestured toward a workbench in the corner of the room. She glanced over and recognized the pages sitting atop the wooden slats.

"They're signed."

"Thank you," she said stiffly, then headed over to retrieve them.

"Wait," Kevin said abruptly and she stopped.

He approached her, his gaze never leaving her face. Cara backed up a few steps. "There's nothing more to say, Kevin."

He pierced her with a sincere look. "How about, I love you. I've never stopped loving you, Cara. But I didn't realize it until last night. I've been a fool and I apologize a hundred times over for how much I've hurt you."

Cara shook her head, unwilling to forgive and forget so easily. "How can I believe you? How can I possibly trust you? You deliberately set out to hurt me. And you succeeded."

Kevin took a few steps closer, his gaze intense. "I'm not going to justify my actions. They were wrong, both then and now. I'd been fooling myself all these years. I let my pride and ego get in the way. We should have talked this out, years ago."

"I'll admit, I probably shouldn't have run away like I did. I was distraught. I didn't know how to get through to you," Cara confessed, finally owning up to her part in their breakup. "And when you didn't come after me, I thought you didn't care anymore."

"Cara, I should have come after you. God knows, I loved you very much. Everything I did was for you. I had something to prove and now I know, I made mistakes along the way. But you have to believe me when I say I'm crazy about you."

Cara let a smile slip out and Kevin smiled, too. "I love you, Cara. And I'll spend the rest of my life proving it to you."

"We're officially divorced now. Unless you lied to me and you didn't sign those papers over there."

"I signed them, to prove how much I love you. If you really want to leave me and Somerset, you can take them and go. But…if there's a chance for us, I want to offer it to you." He made a sweeping gesture with his arm. "This place can be your dance studio, Cara. You can open up Dancing Lights right here in Somerset. I'll build you a house and we'll fill it with children. I want all of that with you. And I'll prove to you every day and night how much you mean to me."

Cara's heart lurched. She could picture a new dance studio here. The place was perfect. More important, she could picture making a home with Kevin…a fresh start. And *children*. Oh, God, he was offering her the sun, the moon and the stars. She wanted to trust him, to believe him.

"I love you, Cara. Do you love me?"

Cara peered into his hopeful, gorgeous blue eyes. "Yes, of course I love you," she said softly. "I've never stopped loving you."

Kevin took her hand in his and squeezed it gently. "Give us a second chance, sweetheart."

Cara smiled. She found the truth in his eyes, the faith

she had in him restored. She walked over to the work-bench and peered down at the signed divorce papers.

"It's up to you, Cara."

Kevin had given her an out. He'd given up control and let the decision rest solely in her hands. He'd let her go if that was what she wanted. But he *loved* her. And she loved him right back.

She picked up the divorce papers. "I don't really have a choice." She ripped them in two, letting the pieces fall to the ground. "I love you too much."

Kevin strode over to her and wrapped her into his arms. His strength and love enveloped her and she knew she'd made the right decision.

They began to sway together.

"Hmm, I hear music," Cara said with a satisfied smile as sweet, joyous music played in her head.

"I hear it every time I hold you." Kevin tightened his arms around her as they rocked gently back and forth. "I can feel the love, sweetheart."

Reminded of their wedding night and the Elton John song that had become their signature, Cara kissed him softly on the lips. "Me, too."

"Promise me one thing, Cara."

"Anything."

"You'll dance for me every night."

"I promise."

And they continued to move to the rhythm of love that played solely in their hearts.

* * * * *

Don't miss next month's
TEXAS CATTLEMAN'S CLUB,
THE OILMAN'S BABY BARGAIN
by Michelle Celmer,
only available from Silhouette Desire.

HARLEQUIN
60 YEARS
of pure reading pleasure

We'll be spotlighting a different series
every month throughout 2009
to celebrate our 60th anniversary.

Look for Silhouette® Nocturne™ in October!

Travel through time to experience tales
that reach the boundaries of life and death.
Bestselling authors Lindsay McKenna, Cindy
Dees, P.C. Cast and Merline Lovelace join
together in a brand-new, four-book
Time Raiders miniseries.

TIME RAIDERS

August—*The Seeker*
by *USA TODAY* bestselling author Lindsay McKenna

September—*The Slayer* by Cindy Dees

October—*The Avenger*
by *New York Times* bestselling author and
coauthor of the House of Night novels P.C. Cast

November—*The Protector*
by *USA TODAY* bestselling author Merline Lovelace

Available wherever books are sold.

nocturne™

New York Times bestselling author
and co-author of the House of Night novels

P.C. CAST

makes her stellar debut
in Silhouette® Nocturne™

THE AVENGER

Available October wherever books are sold.

TIME RAIDERS
miniseries

Bestselling authors Lindsay McKenna,
Cindy Dees, P.C. Cast and Merline Lovelace
come together to bring to life incredible
tales of passion that reach the boundaries
of life and death, in a brand-new
four-book miniseries.

You're invited to join our Tell Harlequin Reader Panel!

By joining our new reader panel you will:

- Receive Harlequin® books—they are FREE and yours to keep with no obligation to purchase anything!
- Participate in fun online surveys
- Exchange opinions and ideas with women just like you
- Have a say in our new book ideas and help us publish the best in women's fiction

In addition, you will have a chance to win great prizes and receive special gifts!
See Web site for details. Some conditions apply.
Space is limited.

To join, visit us at
www.TellHarlequin.com.

REQUEST YOUR FREE BOOKS!

2 FREE NOVELS
PLUS 2
FREE GIFTS!

Passionate, Powerful, Provocative!

YES! Please send me 2 FREE Silhouette Desire® novels and my 2 FREE gifts (gifts are worth about $10). After receiving them, if I don't wish to receive any more books, I can return the shipping statement marked "cancel". If I don't cancel, I will receive 6 brand-new novels every month and be billed just $4.05 per book in the U.S. or $4.74 per book in Canada. That's a savings of almost 15% off the cover price! It's quite a bargain! Shipping and handling is just 50¢ per book.* I understand that accepting the 2 free books and gifts places me under no obligation to buy anything. I can always return a shipment and cancel at any time. Even if I never buy another book, the two free books and gifts are mine to keep forever.   225 SDN EYMS 326 SDN EYM4

Name	(PLEASE PRINT)	
Address		Apt. #
City	State/Prov.	Zip/Postal Code

Signature (if under 18, a parent or guardian must sign)

Mail to the **Silhouette Reader Service:**
IN U.S.A.: P.O. Box 1867, Buffalo, NY 14240-1867
IN CANADA: P.O. Box 609, Fort Erie, Ontario L2A 5X3

Not valid to current subscribers of Silhouette Desire books.

Want to try two free books from another line?
Call 1-800-873-8635 or visit www.morefreebooks.com.

* Terms and prices subject to change without notice. Prices do not include applicable taxes. Sales tax applicable in N.Y. Canadian residents will be charged applicable provincial taxes and GST. Offer not valid in Quebec. This offer is limited to one order per household. All orders subject to approval. Credit or debit balances in a customer's account(s) may be offset by any other outstanding balance owed by or to the customer. Please allow 4 to 6 weeks for delivery. Offer available while quantities last.

Your Privacy: Silhouette Books is committed to protecting your privacy. Our Privacy Policy is available online at www.eHarlequin.com or upon request from the Reader Service. From time to time we make our lists of customers available to reputable third parties who may have a product or service of interest to you. If you would prefer we not share your name and address, please check here. ☐

SDES09R

COMING NEXT MONTH
Available October 13, 2009

#1969 MILLIONAIRE IN COMMAND—Catherine Mann
Man of the Month
This air force captain gets a welcome-home surprise: a pretty stranger caring for a baby with an unquestionable family resemblance—to him! Yet once they marry to secure the child's future, will he want to let his new wife leave his bed?

#1970 THE OILMAN'S BABY BARGAIN—Michelle Celmer
Texas Cattleman's Club: Maverick County Millionaires
Falling for the sexy heiress was unexpected—but not as unexpected as her pregnancy! Though the marriage would be for business, their bedroom deals soon became purely pleasure.

#1971 CLAIMING KING'S BABY—Maureen Child
Kings of California
Their differences over children—she wanted them, he didn't—had this couple on the brink of divorce. Now his wife has come back to his ranch…with their infant son.

#1972 THE BILLIONAIRE'S UNEXPECTED HEIR—Kathie DeNosky
The Illegitimate Heirs
The terms of his inheritance bring this sexy playboy attorney a whole new set of responsibilities…including fatherhood!

#1973 BEDDING THE SECRET HEIRESS—Emilie Rose
The Hightower Affairs
When he hires an heiress as his private pilot, he's determined to find proof she's after a friend's family money. Each suspects the other of having ulterior motives, though neither expected the sparks that fly between them at thirty thousand feet!

#1974 HIS VIENNA CHRISTMAS BRIDE—Jan Colley
Posing as the fiancé of his brother's P.A., the playboy financier is happy to reap the benefits between the sheets…until secrets and a family feud threaten everyone's plans.

SDCNMBPA0909